CRYPTIC BOARDS

GAMES FOUNDER PLAY BEHIND THE HEADLINES

SRINIVAS MAHANKALI

Contents

Preface   v

Acknowledgements   vii

Prologue   ix

  1. Bengaluru, Bootstraps & Big Promises   1

  2. PDFs from Dubai   5

  3. Growth at Any Cost   8

  4. Fault Lines   12

  5. Clockwork Contraband   17

  6. Compliance Bot at 09 : 17   21

  7. Fifty Plants in Fifty Days   26

  8. Shadows Cast Long   29

  9. A Market Made Of Glass   32

10. Acquisition Smells Too Sweet   34

11. Paper Tigers in the C-Suite   37

12. Stock-Manipulation Storm   40

13. Patriot Act Decision - Revisited   43

14. Re-Wiring the Cloud   46

15. Customers Day   49

16. Ransomware Eclipse   51

17. Justice Flight   54

18. Ethics Hackathon   57

19. Margins & Moats   60

20. Prism Crack   63

21. Funding the Beacon   67

22. Storm-Born Clouds   71

23. Wind Against the Glass   75

24. Tainted Wells   79

25. Magnetic Drift   82

Contents

26. Shadow Allies 85

27. Eternal Lease 89

Epilogue 93

Preface

I did not set out to write a thriller. Cryptic Boards is born out of my urge to share my insights as an experienced corporate professionals who worked closely with many founders.

For three decades I have lived the quieter drama of board packs, audit trails, and the green glow of server rooms at 3 a.m. I have served as director, CXO, and, more recently, as a blockchain and cybersecurity evangelist invited to "fix" companies that had already started to crack. Each post-mortem revealed the same pattern: brilliant founders, breathtaking ideas—and a governance vacuum quietly filled by shortcuts. but I knew that the Directors can be the watchdogs, when armed with right tools, can save their companies.

So I began to capture the stories that never reach the press releases: the forged purchase orders slipped in to impress investors; the auditor who okayed a balance sheet after a golf weekend; the security breach hidden for fear of a down-round. To honour confidences, I wove these fragments into fiction. To honour truth, I embedded the controls—open ledgers, dual audits, public escrows—that can turn fragile trust into verifiable fact.

Cryptic Boards is therefore a hybrid: a corporate thriller that aims to entertain, and a field manual for anyone who sits on—or reports to—a board of directors. The characters are inventions; their dilemmas are all too real. If you are a founder, let this book show how rapid growth can invite invisible debts. If you are an investor, use it to sharpen the questions you ask before wiring funds. If you are a regulator or an auditor, treat it as a reminder that sunlight and speed are not enemies.

Most of all, I hope these pages encourage every employee who senses that "something isn't right" to speak, document, and, when necessary, walk away. In an era where a single line of code can trigger a billion-dollar swing, integrity is no longer a moral luxury; it is the ultimate risk-mitigation strategy.

Thank you for opening this book. May the stories within entertain you—and may the lessons help all of us build companies whose ledgers can stand the brightest light.

Srinivas Mahankali

May 2025

Acknowledgements

This book began as a knot of late-night notes on hotel stationery—scribbles born from equal parts frustration and stubborn hope. It would still be a tangle without the people who untied it.

To my family—every patient parent, sibling, spouse, and child who waited while I chased ghosts through boardrooms and code—your quiet faith was the compass that kept me from vanishing into the work.

To friends and colleagues, to the founders and co-founders who invited me into their war rooms, and to the upright board members who led their start-ups and enterprises from the front, thank you for trusting me with your unvarnished stories. Your courage to relive painful chapters gave these pages their pulse.

To the whistle-blowers who whispered "write it down" when silence would have been safer—this book stands on your quiet defiance. I hope its light repays a fraction of your risk.

To the MohSoft team—Sri, Subha, Shyam, and the board, our shared trial by fire proved that transparency is forged, not gifted. May this story honour the resilience you often display at work.

To Shraddha Sharma and the unsung champions at the Ministry of Commerce, your relentless push for a fair and vibrant start-up ecosystem supplied the hope that threads through these chapters.

To my editor, Malathy Singh, who sliced through my jargon with a surgeon's grace and reminded me that a story breathes through characters, not compliance clauses.

To the readers who will underline, question, and perhaps dispute these pages—your scepticism is a gift. Use it in your own boardrooms; let it keep every ledger honest.

And finally, to the founders who dare greatly, may you build companies whose success is measured not only in valuation but in the clarity of the glass that surrounds you. If this book helps even one of you steer clear of the shadows, every lost hour and red-ringed eye will have been worth it.

With gratitude and resolve,
Srinivas Mahankali

Prologue

Two Playbooks, One Dream

The container yard at Nhava Sheva slept under a sodium-yellow haze, its skeletal cranes frozen like prehistoric guardians. It was 3:12 a.m. on the night Shantanu Rao first crossed the line—though he would not admit that for years. The monsoon air smelled of rust, diesel, and wet cardboard, drifting through the half-open window of his rented Mahindra XUV. He tapped the steering wheel in rhythm with his heartbeat: quick, then quicker.

Inside his laptop bag lay six sheets of paper—purchase orders printed on thick ivory stock, stamped with a crimson dragon that read DigiNova Pte. Ltd., Singapore. The dragon looked regal. The signature beneath it looked real. Both were lies Shantanu had invented eleven hours earlier on Photoshop.

He stared at the gates where a lone customs guard dozed in a plastic chair. All he needed was a terminal-yard clerk to sign one manifest, record one container number, and the illusion would be born: SecuComp Group, his fledgling start-up, had just shipped ₹2.8 crore in "IoT gateway appliances" to Southeast Asia. The revenue would hit next quarter's books. Investors, who had been circling like vultures around a too-thin calf, would finally smell meat.

A sudden gust rattled sheet-metal fencing. Shantanu flinched. The guard blinked awake, met Shantanu's eyes across the tarmac, then looked away to light a bidi. Nothing about the moment was cinematic; there was no thunderclap, no moral referee blowing a whistle. Just one man with a laptop bag hoping the night stayed indifferent.

Why am I doing this? The question flickered but failed to ignite remorse. Because if he didn't, the board meeting on Tuesday would collapse into farce. Because one term-sheet from a prestigious fund dangled on the condition of "verifiable export traction." Because payroll was due in nine days. Because other founders were posting growth hacks on LinkedIn while he was triaging invoices. Because, because, because.

His phone buzzed—Telegram, encrypted. "Doc ready?" asked Rajat K. Shantanu's auditor-turned-fellow gambler liked late-night confirmations. He thumbed back: "ETA 20 mins." A blue checkmark appeared instantly. Somewhere in a Bandra high-rise, Rajat was drinking single malt at the firm's expense, blessing numbers he hadn't seen.

Two playbooks, one dream. That phrase had haunted Shantanu since a fireside chat two years earlier when Infosys founder Narayana Murthy told a batch of young entrepreneurs, "There are only two ways to build a company in India: the long road of values, or the shortcut of excuses. Pick once, because you'll wear its consequences forever." The audience had applauded; Shantanu too. Back then, he still believed the long road could be travelled on a seed-stage budget.

The long road was paved by men like Murthy, Azim Premji, and Ratan Tata: stories of refusal to bribe, whistle-blower hotlines, and audits that cut too close to comfort. The shortcut road boasted quicker landmarks: Satyam's phantom cash piles, IL&FS's debt spiral hidden behind glossy annual reports, Nirav Modi's glittering diamond façades. Two playbooks, one dream: success. Tonight, in the dark echo of hydraulic cranes, Shantanu stepped from one script into the other.

He killed the engine, grabbed the bag, and walked toward the administrative block, shoes splashing in monsoon puddles. Every splash sounded louder than the last. Above him, Mumbai's rainclouds glowed with the distant orange of city lights, as if civilisation itself were on slow burn.

Inside, fluorescent tubes hummed over dented metal desks. A clerk with pan-red teeth looked up, annoyed at the intrusion. Shantanu placed the manifest and forged purchase orders on the counter with hands that refused to shake. "Urgent export filing," he said. "Customer penalty clause if container misses the morning vessel."

Pan-stained lips curled. "Overtime charge, boss."

"Already accounted," Shantanu said, sliding across an envelope of crisp ₹500 notes—legitimate this time. The clerk weighed the envelope with the elegance of a jeweller, then stamped each document without reading. The noise of rubber meeting paper was shockingly loud, like a judge's gavel striking over and over.

Thud.

SecuComp had revenue.

Thud.

Shantanu had traction.

Thud.

The shortcut had begun.

He stepped back into the rain, heartbeat steady now. The guard at the gate slept again. Mumbai's distant skyline shimmered—a hologram of opportunity built on credit and optimism. He thought of Devika Sinha, the independent director who'd joined SecuComp's board last quarter, a former Tata Steel executive with eyes that sliced excuses. Devika would ask to see shipping proofs; she always asked for proofs. But proofs could be manufactured. The auditor would vouch; investors would cheer; the media would crave the next Bengaluru unicorn.

Shantanu slid into the driver's seat, wiped rain off his glasses, and caught his reflection in the rear-view mirror. For a fleeting second he didn't recognise the man staring back. The mirror held the version of him that pitched sustainability, transparency, and "building for Bharat." The man with the bag full of inventions belonged elsewhere—maybe in one of those true-crime business podcasts he used to devour on long flights.

He turned the key. The diesel grumbled awake. As the vehicle rolled out of the yard, his phone pinged again—this time a push alert: **"BREAKING: BYJU'S valued at \$22 billion in new round."** Commentators on social media were already typing India Shining with rocket emojis. Shantanu laughed, not at the headline but at how perfectly timed the universe could be when it wanted to join in the joke.

Across the city, in an apartment lit by a single desk lamp, Devika Sinha couldn't sleep. She had spent the evening revisiting SecuComp's draft accounts, the rows of revenue lines too symmetrical, the margin curve too smooth for a hardware-heavy early-stage firm. Her phone rested face-down to avoid the glow of incoming congratulatory messages from friends who'd seen her photo in a business magazine: "Meet the Woman Guiding India's Next Tech Star." She felt less guide, more reluctant passenger on a train whose speed she didn't control.

Devika reached for a notebook titled Board Questions – SecuComp. On the first empty page she wrote Export Receivables – Proof? Underlined twice. She closed the book, turned off the lamp, and lay in darkness listening to the rain drum her balcony grill. Sleep remained elusive. Somewhere in the night, a founder she admired was making a choice that would soon demand an answer from her conscience.

At 5:47 a.m., Shantanu's car entered Bengaluru city limits. Dawn leaked grey and pink over the Outer Ring Road flyovers. Tech-park billboards flashed DIGITAL TRANSFORMATION OR DIE. He parked outside SecuComp's modest office suite, shoulders aching, but adrenaline intact. Inside, junior engineers would arrive in an hour to polish code that still crashed under load tests. They would never know their pay-checks now relied on six forged pieces of paper drying in his laptop bag.

In the lobby, he passed a framed quote he'd chosen on Day One: "Integrity is doing the right thing when no one is watching." — C.S. Lewis. He paused, considered ripping it off the wall, then walked on. Better to leave it. Every cathedral needs its stained-glass irony.

The sun crested over glass towers, casting long shadows that made the campus look twice its size. Shantanu set the bag on his desk, exhaled, and drafted an email to his investors: "Thrilled to report a landmark export shipment validating global demand for our IoT stack. Details in attached manifest. Next steps: scale."

He hit send. In that silent moment, he felt something equal parts giddy and hollow—like standing at the top of a carnival ride hearing the gears click forward, knowing gravity would soon take over. He told himself he could always step off; this was just a bridge loan from morality, payable in full once real orders arrived.

Outside, the city roared awake. Inside, the carousel took its first turn. And in the quiet space between heartbeat and breath, the stage was set for a story that would drag auditors into courtrooms, topple share prices, and force a nation obsessed with unicorns to confront the cost of borrowed glitter.

Two playbooks. One dream. The first move had been made. Everything else would follow its ledger.

CHAPTER ONE

Bengaluru, Bootstraps & Big Promises

Shantanu Rao's first glimpse of Bengaluru's dawn was always from the pillion seat of a bike-taxi that shot past stalled autos like a silver bullet. 5:27 a.m.—the hour when Outer Ring Road looked less like a clogged artery and more like a runway of neon. Half-finished towers loomed overhead, their cranes frozen mid-gesture, as if the city had been caught bragging in its sleep.

The driver—helmet scarred, raincoat flapping—leaned back and yelled through the wind, "Start-up loge sab pagal, sir! Night shift over but you still going to office?"

"Dreams don't keep office hours," Shantanu shouted back, though the words tasted like an energy-drink advertisement even to him.

They swung onto the service lane that fed **LaunchPad Coworks**, a glass-and-concrete hive jammed between a chain hotel and a half-illegal dosa cart. A vinyl banner outside screamed "**HIRING FULL-STACK NINJAS – EQUITY, COFFEE, PURPOSE!**" Two pigeons, fat on leftover vada crumbs, pecked at the exclamation point.

Inside, badge scanners beeped like slot machines. Coders in hoodies dozed on beanbags, MacBooks balanced on their chests. Someone's Spotify playlist pushed out lo-fi beats that smelled of desperation and mango e-liquid. On the far wall, a giant counter glowed ?? **108 UNICORNS AND COUNTING**—three more than yesterday, according to the algorithm that scraped valuation news faster than truth could stiffen its spine.

Shantanu ducked into SecuComp's four-desk corner—a kingdom marked by a taped logo and a rented ficus. "Morning, Chief," mumbled Amit the firmware lead, hair sticking up like a question mark. He hadn't been home.

None of them had. The sprint to demo-day was a treadmill angled at forty-five degrees.

Shantanu dropped two cardboard cups on the desk. "Cold brew for you, optimism for me."

Amit sipped, winced. "Tastes like burnt tyres."

"Growth always does."

Bengaluru's New Gold Rush

Someone once told him that Silicon Valley was built on optimism; Bengaluru, on revenge. Revenge against a system that rewarded rote learning, against government banks that asked for collateral before ideas, against relatives who measured worth in either IIT ranks or secured marriages. Here, ambition was caffeine and FOMO its creamer.

Flipkart had shown the path, Byju's had paved it with cash, and the venture funds now arrived in chartered jets, passing out term-sheets like festival sweets—provided you already looked inevitable. To look inevitable you needed traction; to get traction you needed customers; to get customers you sometimes needed to pretend you already had traction. Circular logic, but circles spin fast.

Shantanu's calendar overflowed with pitch invitations: "Be the AWS of manufacturing," "Digitise India's smokestacks," "Solve latency, own destiny." Investors devoured buzzwords like schoolkids inhaling pani-puri. He'd memorised the script: Say "Bharat," nod to Industry 4.0, sprinkle ESG, promise an IPO slide. Close strong with TAM so huge it needed commas the way palaces needed chandeliers.

What he lacked was time. Payroll thundered closer; the landlord had begun emailing in all caps. So nights grew longer, and the moral grey stretched lighter until it looked almost white.

The Myth Factory

At 7:12 a.m. a Slack notification pinged: **Nisha Jain → #hiring**.

<Got two resumes from IIT-D. Both want 3× salary + ESOP!>

Shantanu typed: <Tell them equity today, Tesla tomorrow. If they hesitate, they're tourists.> He added a rocket emoji, because in start-up land sincerity travelled best by pictogram.

He opened the day's news feed:

ZippPay bags $75 M Series B at $700 M

AgroByte to acquire rival in part-stock deal

Government mulls stricter checks on overseas funding

The first two headlines inflated Shantanu's lungs; the third pierced them. Stricter checks meant slower dollars, meant VCs would start asking grown-up questions. He closed the tab before anxiety could metastasise.

Amit wheeled over. "Sensor calibration's drifting. We need better op-amps."

"Can we patch in software?"

"Not unless physics accepts a pull-request, boss."

Shantanu laughed too loudly. "Then we pray physics is in beta."

Koshy's Café, 10:23 a.m.

Deal discussions in Bengaluru resembled arranged-marriage first meets: stiff smiles, guarded flirtation, an unspoken ledger of dowry and deliverables. Shantanu slid into a wooden booth across from Varun Gupta, junior associate at Frontier Capital, hair parted like a Silicon Alley banker.

Varun checked his Apple Watch. "So, Shantanu, pitch me the dream in one breath."

"One platform, four million machines, zero downtime," Shantanu exhaled.

Varun typed something. "Sounds like 'AWS for factories.'"

Shantanu grinned. "Only better margins than Amazon."

Varun's eyes glittered—moths to vanity's flame. "You'll need proof of scale."

"Three pilots live, export demand warming." A half-truth tastes harmless if swallowed quickly.

Varun nodded. "Send me monthly recurring numbers by Sunday. If the curve smiles, Frontier smiles."

Outside, church bells clanged noon. Shantanu paid the bill with a credit card already chewing through its last available rupee and walked out onto St. Mark's Road feeling eight feet tall and hollow inside.

Tilted Runway

Back at LaunchPad, the team prepped for the evening stand-up. Charts opened like casino floors: CAC down (massaged), MRR up (forecast), churn flat (ignored). The dopamine hit was immediate; the blind spots, terminal.

Shantanu ended with a fist-pump. "Remember, India doesn't reward the cautious. It rewards the courageous."

A junior engineer muttered, "Or the crooked." Not loud enough to matter.

Lights dimmed, laptops glowed, and the night jumped tracks. Miriam in marketing wrote blog posts about "decentralised edge-intelligence." Ravi in sales spammed LinkedIn contacts with "limited founder-pricing." Amit hacked the firmware until code blurred into static.

At 2:03 a.m. Shantanu stood alone on the terrace, city lights shimmering like crushed diamonds. He imagined every bulb was a potential sensor his gateways would someday monitor. The fantasy warmed him more than the stale filter coffee in his hand.

Then his phone pinged—a reminder: **INVESTOR UPDATE D-5 → export revenue evidence.** Cold reality sluiced down his spine. DigiNova was still just a dragon-logo in a folder. The investors would want more than logos; they'd want ledgers. And ledgers needed ink.

He pictured a container yard bathed in sodium streetlight, imagined steel boxes branded with SecuComp's logo rolling onto a cargo vessel bound for Singapore. He could almost smell the diesel, feel the humidity.

A choice flickered: wait for actual orders—or manufacture a preview of destiny?

In the distance, thunder mumbled. Bengaluru's first monsoon shower of the season would hit before dawn, washing dust from glass facades and hope from tired sidewalks. He wondered which would vanish first: the grime or his conscience.

"Just one invoice," he whispered. "One little push to tip the dominoes."

The sky answered with lightning that forked across the plateau like a signature etched in fire.

Shantanu pocketed his phone, headed downstairs, and opened Photoshop.

The unicorn counter in the lobby clicked up to **109**. Somewhere, someone else had convinced the world of a future still under construction. Bengaluru applauded. Shantanu typed.

The hustle had found its next volunteer.

CHAPTER TWO

PDFs from Dubai

A single keystroke can feel like a crime.

At 1:43 a.m., with thunder rattling the LaunchPad windows, Shantanu Rao pressed Save as PDF—and SecuComp's destiny changed fonts.

The Dragon with No Address

He began by sketching a logo: a crimson dragon coiled round a printed-circuit disc. It looked credible in the way most tech logos do—minimalist, vaguely Eastern, rich enough to whisper "Series B." Beneath it he typed:

DigiNova Pte. Ltd.

15 Tuas South Avenue 8

Singapore 637021

The address was a mail-drop box he'd rented online for 29 Singapore dollars. The registrar threw in a voicemail line that forwarded to a Google number routed straight to archive. If investors ever dialled, they'd meet infinite ring-tone.

Next he duplicated a free Canva invoice template:

| **Invoice** No. | DN-SC-0801 |

| **Date** | 15 Aug 20xx |

| **Buyer** | DigiNova Pte. Ltd. |

| **Seller** | SecuComp Technologies Pvt. Ltd. |

| **Item** | EdgeSight™ IoT Gateway (220 units) |

| **Unit Price** | USD 2,600 |

| **Total** | USD 572,000 |

Freight, insurance and an "expedited deployment service" nudged the figure past ₹5 crore—the milestone his VCs demanded.

Shantanu signed for "Calvin Tan, Procurement Head" with a sleek cursive script. Calvin Tan was real, sort of—an ex-roommate's cousin who once owed Shantanu ₹3,000 for biryani packets. Debt forgiven, identity borrowed.

Container #TCNU-49113270

Export paperwork is usually a bureaucratic marathon. Shantanu ran a 100-metre dash in the sandbox mode of ICEGATE—the customs portal meant for software testers. He uploaded a dummy manifest, clicked Submit, screen-captured the "Successful Filing" banner, Photoshopped a ₹200 "duty paid" stamp, and closed the tab before the site's clock ticked to 03:00.

For good measure he dragged a stock photo of an Evergreen container into the folder, renamed it TCNU-49113270.jpeg, and called the job done.

Inside **"DigiNova-Export-Bundle.zip"** now lay:

1. Commercial Invoice
2. Purchase Order
3. Packing List
4. Customs Acknowledgment
5. Container Image
6. A hope big enough to drown conscience

Auditor on Speed-Dial

At 2:27 a.m. WhatsApp vibrated: **Rajat K. (Audit Partner)**
Docs tonight? IC meets 10 a.m. Tokyo.

Shantanu shot him the ZIP. Rajat's reply was a lone ?— auditor-speak for plausible enough. An hour later, Rajat would e-mail an "unmodified opinion" draft. Lesson from Satyam: never question too loudly when fees are prompt.

Devika Detects the Dragon

Twenty kilometres away, **Devika Sinha**—SecuComp's only truly independent director—skimmed the same PDFs during her 6:15 a.m. Metro ride. Something felt off: why would a Singapore SME import 220 high-end gateways for a pilot?

She circled the container number in her notebook, scribbled **"Verify on Maersk Tracker."** Old-school governance rarely slept.

The Echo Chamber Ignites

By 10 a.m. Shantanu's blast-mail hit investor inboxes:

Thrilled to announce our first multi-crore export to ASEAN smart factories. P&L impact: ₹5.2 cr topline, 47 % GM. Full roll-out Q4. ?

Replies arrived in minutes:

- "Phenomenal—looping Asia Growth desk."
- "Series B convo ASAP?"
- "Proud backers of the next deep-tech unicorn!"

Slack erupted in confetti GIFs. HR stapled the news to the pantry corkboard. Shantanu watched likes mount on LinkedIn, each click another brick in his papier-mâché castle.

A City Cannot Hear a Canary

Headlines scrolled in the lobby ticker:

- **IL&FS founders arrested in ₹91,000 cr scam**
- **NFRA fines PwC ₹23 cr for Satyam lapses**
- **Byju's revenue recognition under SEBI lens**

Warnings flashed like ambulance lights, but the party music inside Koramangala drowned sirens. Shantanu opened Gmail, drafted a fake SWIFT MT103 "in-transit remittance," and promised himself reality would catch up before auditors did.

Midnight Rain

Lightning split the sky as he locked the office. Water pooled in potholes, mirroring a billboard that roared **BUILD THE FUTURE**. The reflection rippled—letters warping, re-forming. He stepped around the puddle, unwilling to disturb the illusion.

Behind him, the neon unicorn counter inside LaunchPad clicked from 109 to 110. Another founder, somewhere, had sold tomorrow today.

Shantanu breathed the petrichor, clutched his laptop like a talisman, and whispered, "Just a bridge loan from the future."

Thunder answered, low and knowing.

CHAPTER THREE

Growth at Any Cost

Rain sluiced down the glass façade of LaunchPad Coworks, turning Bengaluru's dawn into a watercolor smear of tail-lights and turmeric-yellow auto-rickshaws. Inside SecuComp's corner bay, LED strips glowed electric blue, casting the team's faces in a submarine pallor. A poster of a rocket—its plume rendered in glossy crimson—dominated the back wall, shouting "MOONSHOT OR BUST."

Shantanu Rao stood beneath it like a preacher at the pulpit. His reflection in the glass door multiplied—one man cloned into half a dozen by the angled panes—an accidental metaphor for the double lives he now lived.

1 ▪ KPI Graffiti

Whiteboards flanking the war-room bore a frenzy of marker strokes: green arrows stabbed skyward; red triangles warned of "runway burn"; a cartoon goat—SecuComp's unofficial mascot—wore sunglasses beside the phrase **G.O.A.T. METRICS.**

Shantanu tapped the board three times.
"Team, welcome to 10-10-10 season."

₹10 crore monthly bookings—he underlined the figure until the marker squeaked.

10 percent churn cap—a modest plateau painted in pastel purple, as if attrition could be tamed by color choice.

10 new logos a quarter—each would become a trophy decal on the website's hero strip.

A projector blasted the roadmap across the wall: sprint lanes glimmered like a Formula 1 circuit; each milestone crown-badged in gold. The engineers squinted, pupils contracting at the overdose of optimism.

2 ▪ Investors in 4K

Two days later, the conference room morphed into a film set. Potted palms appeared; a rented 4K camera perched on a tripod; ring lights traced halos around Shantanu's silhouette. The visiting VCs—block-printed shirts, minimalist sneakers—sat at a reclaimed-wood table scattered with single-origin espresso cups.

On the screen behind him, a digital twin of an Indonesian cement plant rotated slowly—dust clouds rendered as soft-focus particles. Gauges pulsed green; an animated forklift glided along a track so smooth it looked sorcerous.

"EdgeSight dashboards shrink downtime by 38 percent," Shantanu narrated, swiping mid-air like a weather anchor. The slide advanced to a graph whose teal bars vaulted higher than a city skyline.

Varun Gupta from Frontier Capital leaned forward; the ring light caught flecks of gold in his tortoiseshell frames. "Impressive. How soon to triple deployment?"

"Two quarters—assuming Series B closes." Shantanu smiled, teeth reflecting the slide's neon.

Outside the fishbowl, junior developers pressed against the glass, watching the theatre of millions unfurl.

3 ▪ The Pipeline Mirage

Every Friday, Sales Head Prabhu "Pipeline" Nair commandeered the all-hands. His laser pointer darted like a firefly across a mammoth monitor displaying S-1 LEADS—each dot a prospective deal. The Asia-Pacific cluster shimmered crimson, dense as chilli flakes on a dosa.

"Forty-eight active pilots!" he crowed. The screen zoomed into heat-map mode; faux customer logos glowed lava-red over Singapore, Jakarta, Ho Chi Minh. If maps could mint revenue, SecuComp was already richer than SAP.

An intern in the back whispered, "S-1 just means they asked for a brochure." Another shushed him; the cult of momentum brooked no heresy.

4 ▪ Cash-Flow Cirque du Soleil

In Finance, beige cubicles were replaced by glossy white desks under strip-lights bright enough to blanch skin. Spreadsheet waterfalls cascaded across dual monitors. Cobalt FX invoices—vendor ghosts—floated between folders like unbidden spirits.

Controller Meera Deshpande flipped her mouse, scrolling through a pivot table taller than the office Christmas tree. Payables deferred, receivables imagined, GST offsets spun like acrobats. Above her desk hung a motivational plaque: "LIQUIDITY IS LIFEBLOOD." The liquidity in question was a river of IOUs.

Rajat the auditor breezed in, cologne sharp, suit darker than compliance midnight. He pointed to a line item labelled Unbilled Revenue (DigiNova). "Round that to nearest lakh," he murmured. "Symmetry sells."

Meera's fingers hesitated. "We're billing the future, sir."

"Then let's make the future photogenic."

5 ▪ Culture Under Neon

Human Resources turned the sixth-floor breakout into a photo-booth corner: ring-light, fake grass, cardboard cut-outs of Elon Musk and a Shiba Inu. New hires posed clutching signs: "I CODE, THEREFORE I AM"; "SLEEP = LEGACY TECH." The carousel of smiles found its way onto LinkedIn, each post tagged #LifeAtSecuComp.

Behind the selfies: electrolyte sachets, eye-drops, a sofa where Amit—the firmware lead—cat-napped under a silver emergency blanket. Once he jolted awake, VR headset askew, mumbling PWM duty cycles. A banner overhead declared "HUSTLE IS THE NEW CHILL."

6 ▪ Red Flags in Monsoon Blue

Evening rain crept into cable trenches, flickering lights. Power dipped; UPS fans shrieked. Devika Sinha's stiletto heels clicked across the damp marble as she arrived for the quarterly board call. She carried no laptop—only a Moleskine, its edges bristling with neon tabs.

The video wall hummed to life. Directors in different time-zones framed themselves against curated backdrops: leather-bound books, vintage Fender guitars, a Himalayan trekking poster. Devika's feed showed a plain grey wall.

Shantanu presented the Series B term-sheet: ₹160 crore headline, ₹ 750-crore pre-money. Fireworks animation erupted on-screen—gold sparks showering the term-sheet PDF like digital Diwali.

Devika waited for silence then slid a photograph onto the shared screen: a corrugated door stamped 15 Tuas South Ave 8. The lock was rusted; no dragon logo in sight.

"This is DigiNova's registered office," she said softly. The silence that followed was heavier than thunder.

Rajat adjusted his tie. "Virtual offices are standard in Singapore—tax efficiency, flexible leasing..."

Devika's eyes never left Shantanu. "Thirty days. Show us bank advice of export proceeds, or I file a dissent with SEBI." The word dissent echoed off the conference-room's tempered glass like a gavel strike.

The meeting ended; fireworks froze mid-spark.

7 ▪ Decision at the Parapet

Midnight. Rain had polished the rooftop tiles into obsidian mirrors. Shantanu stood at the parapet, neon signage from neighbouring towers washing his face in candy hues—pink, jade, electric tangerine. Below, the city murmured: bike horns, temple bells, EDM bass leaking from a rooftop bar four blocks away.

In his pocket buzzed the Series B draft—wealth for employees, exits for early angels, vindication in headlines. In his head replayed Devika's ultimatum; in his gut coiled a dragon breathing spreadsheets of fire.

Lightning spider-webbed the sky, revealing for an instant the jagged silhouette of crane arms and half-built condos. He felt like one of those skeleton towers: impressive against the sky, hollow inside, waiting for concrete—or collapse.

He whispered to the wind, "After this raise, truth will catch up. We'll earn the numbers."

The wind did not reply. But somewhere a loose hoarding flapped like a slow hand-clap.

Shantanu turned away from the parapet, shoes squelching on rain-slick tile, and headed downstairs to his office.

The elevator doors slid shut, severing the rooftop's panorama. Inside the metal box, his reflection stared back—suit drenched at the shoulders, eyes bright with adrenaline, jaw set in reckless conviction.

One floor above Finance, the LED ticker outside LaunchPad's lobby blinked from ₹99,992,000 to ₹100,000,000 in venture inflows recorded city-wide. A perfect, round vanity milestone for Bengaluru. The number glowed a triumphant gold before dissolving into the next stat.

Growth had been fed—for tonight.

CHAPTER FOUR

Fault Lines

The Series B term-sheet spread through SecuComp's Slack like caffeine in an IV drip. Emojis detonated in channels—?, ?, ?—a digital sky-show of premature victory. Yet beneath the confetti codebase, tension hair-line-fractured every department. Some cracks were loud; most were silent, widening in the dark.

1 ▪ Engineering Debt, Interest Compounding

Amit's firmware team now lived on gummy bears and resignation letters half-drafted but never sent. The new sprint board—projected in 110-inch 4K—looked less like an agile roadmap and more like an ECG of someone on the brink of cardiac arrest: spikes, crashes, flatlines.

At 03:12 a.m., a junior dev pushed a hot-fix that short-circuited the gateway's temperature sensor. An alarm script mis-read the $-273\,°C$ value as "hardware idle," auto-shutting five pilot units on a factory floor in Hosur. Production halted; the plant manager left a voicemail in abrasive Tamil, suggesting that EdgeSight find the nearest trash can.

Shantanu ordered the voicemail archived. "We'll handle Hosur after Series B closes," he told Amit, who stared at his terminal like a hostage negotiator pleading with an unstable captor—the code.

2 ▪ Investor Shadow-Boxing

Frontier Capital's US partners demanded a fresh data room, three-day turnaround. Shantanu fed them a curated zoo of metrics—MAU graphs smoothed by logarithmic scale, pipeline screenshots with S-1s labelled "active pilots," gleaming testimonials signed Calvin Tan.

But investors are sharks: taste one drop of off-color hemoglobin and they circle. A visiting analyst from Boston ran DigiNova's container number through the Maersk tracker; status returned "Not Found." He emailed back a mild query flagged Low Importance—the kind of digital whisper that signals a scream a week later.

Rajat replied first, cc'ing Shantanu:

"Customs trans-shipment delay—common in ASEAN lanes. Updated docs imminent."

Imminent in audit-speak usually means invented. The analyst accepted—for now. Sharks sometimes snooze.

3 ▪ Devika's Quiet Volcano

Devika Sinha had spent two decades spotting rot beneath marble. She started her mornings at the old Bangalore Club, nursing filter coffee and reading investigative footnotes like others read horoscopes. The day after the board call she rang an ex-colleague now posted at the Monetary Authority of Singapore (MAS).

Ten minutes later her notebook held three bullets:

DigiNova Pte. Ltd. – **no goods-and-services filings**

Virtual mailbox renewed quarterly with prepaid Visa card

Calvin Tan – LinkedIn empty since 2017

Devika slid the notebook across her desk, the neon tabs fluttering like warning flags. She drafted a two-page letter to SEBI's Corporate Finance Department, saved it in Drafts, and waited.

4 ▪ Meera's Fork in the Ledger

In Finance, Controller Meera Deshpande stared at a flashing cursor in Tally ERP. Rajat needed her to book a back-dated Forex gain on DigiNova's "incoming remittance." The entry would plug a ₹48-lakh gap and tidy the half-year P&L.

Meera's father, a retired bank manager, had taught her one rule: Entries fade, but signatures stay. She hovered over the keyboard. Then she opened WhatsApp, scrolled to her college mentor, typed:

Ever been asked to back-date export proceeds?

The reply arrived as two emojis: ??.

Her pulse banged against her eardrums. She closed Tally without saving.

5 ▪ Smoke Test

Shantanu scheduled a visit to the Hosur plant to "re-instill customer confidence." He hired a PR videographer to document the handshake. The night before, Amit patched the firmware bug with a 'null suppression layer'—essentially telling the sensor to ignore temperatures below −10 °C.

At Hosur, factory heat hovered near 55 °C. The gateways lit green for the camera crew. The plant manager crossed his arms, sceptical. But the footage—angled just right—would splice seamlessly into a case-study montage. Perception restored.

On the drive back, Shantanu's phone buzzed: Varun Gupta.

"HQ wants a site visit next fortnight—tech & finance diligence. And Calvin Tan will join via Zoom. That okay?"

Shantanu's throat tightened. Calvin Tan was a paper doll; Zoom required flesh.

"Perfect," he said. "We'll roll out the red carpet."

6 ▪ Summoning the Dragon

That night he dialled Singapore via WhatsApp. A drowsy voice answered.

"Bro, you know it's 2 a.m.?" It was the real Calvin, now a med-tech sales rep.

"I need a favour," Shantanu began.

When he finished explaining, Calvin's line went silent except for ceiling-fan whir.

"That's... shady, man."

"I'll wire fifteen grand. One hour on Zoom, read a script. No questions."

Calvin sighed. "I still owe you that three grand."

"Call it paid—with interest."

"Fine. But blur my last name."

Shantanu exhaled. The dragon had acquired vocal cords.

7 ▪ Day of the Downpour

On diligence day, Bengaluru's sky resembled wet slate. Frontier Capital's entourage arrived in frontier-chic Patagonia jackets. The lobby receptionist handed them mango-flavored welcome shots dotted with chia. Upstairs, the office smelled of new carpet; housekeeping had spritzed lemongrass to mask solder fumes.

The demo began—laser pointers slicing data-flows; dashboards rippling teal and sunshine-yellow. At 10:00 a.m. sharp, Calvin appeared on the 70-inch screen: collar crisp, virtual background of a Singapore skyline at dusk. He read from the teleprompter Shantanu had embedded in Zoom's screen share.

Varun nodded, taking notes. The Boston analyst, however, tilted her head, narrowing her eyes at Calvin's backdrop. At 10:07 she clicked 'View Original' on the background. A faint watermark emerged: **FREEPIX PREMIUM TRIAL.**

Her eyebrow rose.

8 ▪ Seismic Sound

The diligence wrapped with courteous applause. Investors filed out, rain drumming on their umbrellas like anxious fingertips. Shantanu retreated to the war-room, chest tight.

At 4:32 p.m. his phone chimed:

Need clarification on DigiNova remittance. Share bank advice by EOD tomorrow. —Varun

Shantanu glanced at Meera's cubicle. She was gone; her drawer hung open, ID lanyard coiled like a discarded question mark.

A second message pinged—Devika.

Dinner? 8 p.m. Residency Road. Non-negotiable.

He read it twice. The building's HVAC hummed like distant thunder. Fault lines, once hair-thin, now yawned.

9 ▪ Supper of Reckoning

Residency Road's traffic honked medieval horns. In an ivy-covered bistro, Devika stirred her lime soda with clinical patience. Shantanu arrived soaked, heart thrashing.

She slid a folder across: DigiNova filings, mailbox receipts, MAS print-outs.

"I haven't sent it yet," she said. "But if you fake bank advice, I will."

Outside the window, lightning forked over UB Tower, illuminating raindrops into spears of glass.

Shantanu's shoulders sagged. "It started as a bridge to survive. Now it's a bridge on fire."

"Blow it out," Devika said. "Or burn with it."

10 ▪ Knife-Edge

Midnight found Shantanu alone in the office, city lights veiled by monsoon mist. On one monitor: Rajat pleading via Zoom to "just fabricate the SWIFT once." On another: Varun's email. On a third: Devika's folder, scanned, pages lined like indictment bars.

He opened Tally, stared at DigiNova Receivable – USD 572,000. His finger hovered over DELETE. Outside, thunder cracked so loud it rattled ceiling tiles.

The screen reflected in his pupils—a forked road. Press Delete and watch the castle crumble; press Duplicate and erect another façade.

In the silence between thunderclaps, he whispered a decision only the servers heard.

The herbal air-freshener hissed again, masking the smell of ozone.

Far below, in the rain-slicked street, a neon billboard flickered: **TRUTH IS A DEADLINE.**

Its last bulb died, plunging the slogan—and perhaps SecuComp—into blackout.

CHAPTER FIVE

Clockwork Contraband

The monsoon clouds that draped Bengaluru looked less like weather and more like judgement. Shantanu Rao had seventy-two hours to turn a phantom export into a breathing, billable order—or watch SecuComp collapse under the weight of its own fiction.

1 ▪ Seventy-Two-Hour Plan

T - 72 hrs – Thursday, 09:00

War-room lights snapped on. Shantanu unrolled a paper map of Southeast Asia, pins already stabbed into Singapore, Jakarta, and Ho Chi Minh.

"Target: **TransAstra-SG**—a scrappy industrial-automation distributor in Jurong," he announced. "They demoed EdgeSight six months ago, loved it, couldn't afford it. We give them hero pricing, twenty-percent deposit upfront, ninety-day credit on balance."

Amit raised an eyebrow. "At that discount we bleed."

"We bleed red to live through Friday," Shantanu shot back.

Meera, coaxed back by a promise of legality, murmured, "I'll prep a clean invoice dated tomorrow—no backdating. Deposit must hit ICICI NOSTRO by Saturday 5 p.m.; anything later and the SWIFT won't post before Varun's deadline."

Devika, still neutral, leaned against the doorway. "Get written board consent to discount that deep, or I don't sign."

"Draft it," Shantanu said, "I'll collect e-signatures mid-flight."

2 ▪ Red-Eye to Reality

T - 60 hrs – Thursday, 21:15

Kempegowda T1. Shantanu and Amit boarded an Indigo red-eye, hand-carrying two showcase gateways wrapped in anti-static film. Cabin lights dimmed; Shantanu's laptop glowed with a pitch deck re-branded overnight: "EdgeSight-Lite — Pay-As-You-Scale."

A seatbelt sign pinged off. Shantanu opened WhatsApp:

Shantanu: Board consent doc sent. Need sign within 6 hrs.

Devika: I'll sign when deposit lands.

3 ▪ Jurong Bargain

T - 46 hrs – Friday, 11:30 (SGT)

TransAstra's warehouse smelled of diesel and durian from the hawker centre next-door. CEO Leon Ng—all buzz-cut and sleeve tattoos—eyed the demo unit like contraband.

"USD 2,600 list, you give me for 900?" he scoffed.

"Introductory," Shantanu lied smoothly, "Because Singapore is our ASEAN lighthouse."

Leon drummed fingers on a forklift crate. "Twenty-percent deposit, you ship twenty units Monday. Rest after field test."

Shantanu extended a hand. "Deal."

Meera, on Teams audio, whispered through AirPods: "Invoice sent. They must TT by 4 p.m. local to clear Indian banking cut-off."

4 ▪ The Thunderclap Transfer

T - 39 hrs – Friday, 18:02 (IST)

ICICI's NOSTRO queue closed at six. At 18:02 the SWIFT terminal chimed: USD 3 600 remitted – Value 3 585 after fees. Not the ₹48 lakh Shantanu hoped for—but enough to replace the forged advice with a real, if smaller, one.

Meera's text: Funds landed. Uploading MT103.

Devika's signature pinged the consent doc one minute later.

5 ▪ Chicken-Run Logistics

T - 32 hrs – Friday, 23:30

Bengaluru airport cargo – Customs night shift. Shantanu used *'his charm'* a freight forwarder to bump twenty gateways (HS-Code falsely tagged as "Low-power sensors") onto a Saturday DHL freighter.

The forwarder warned, "I can flag them 'radio-exempt', but Singapore might inspect."

"Just get them airborne," Shantanu said, signing the manifest with a hand that only trembled after the pen left paper.

6 ▪ Banker's Daylight

T - 18 hrs – Saturday, 14:10

Meera uploaded the genuine MT103 to Frontier Capital's data room: "Customer Deposit – EdgeSight Pilot, TransAstra-SG." She highlighted the remitting bank's stamp, praying analysts wouldn't note the modest sum.

Varun replied in 22 minutes: Good start. Proof of shipment?

Shantanu forwarded the DHL AWB, hoping the plane was already over the Andaman Sea.

7 ▪ Sky-Check at Changi

T - 12 hrs – Saturday, 20:05 (SGT)

Changi Cargo Terminal. Leon live-streamed the pallet unload to Shantanu: brown cartons labelled "Demo – Not For Resale." Customs sealed them pending "RF compliance verification"—a 48-hour hold.

Leon texted: Customs want Conformity Certification.

Amit cursed in the cab back in Bengaluru. "We never cleared Singapore SRRC."

Shantanu's mind raced: No release, no final boarding pass to legitimacy.

8 ▪ Ghost Certificate Gambit

T - 8 hrs – Saturday, 22:15 (IST)

Rajat, cornered in his apartment, opened a dusty folder: an old CE compliance report from an obsolete Wi-Fi module vendor—names different, frequencies close. They swapped logos in Acrobat, output a crisp PDF hallmarked "IMDA Approved".

Meera hesitated. "Forgery again?"

"Placeholder," Shantanu pleaded. "Actual cert in four weeks. This tides us over 48 hours."

Devika, on speaker, sighed. "I'll pretend I didn't hear that. Miss the Monday board call and I walk to SEBI."

9 ▪ Investor Deadline

T - 0 hrs – Sunday, 06:59

Frontier Capital's Boston analyst logged into the data room. Shipment AWB: scanned. IMDA certificate: present. MT103: verified. She typed a note: Red-flag earlier cleared – pilot revenue confirmed.

Varun emailed Shantanu:

Congrats. IC signs off. Series B terms move to legal docs.

Shantanu exhaled—a sound between prayer and exhaust leak.

10 ▪ Calm or Eye of Storm?

Sunday night. LaunchPad's rooftop, rain finally spent, city lights shimmering like embers. Amit clinked a paper coffee cup against Shantanu's.

"Pulled it off, Chief. For real this time."

Shantanu watched a plane's strobes blink westward—possibly the same freighter heading home. "For real enough," he said.

Far below, a scooter splashed through puddles. Its taillight left a fleeting red smear, like someone striking a match in the dark.

Shantanu pocketed his phone, unaware that IMDA's compliance bot would flag the doctored certificate at 09:17 Monday, auto-emailing a query to Singapore Customs and CC-ing MAS.

Some victories last a quarter. Some, exactly 26 hours and 18 minutes.

The clock had started again.

CHAPTER SIX

Compliance Bot at 09:17

The Singapore dawn rose white-hot and clinical, like a surgical lamp over the gleaming cranes of Tuas. Inside the Infocomm Media Development Authority's data-center, a routine batch job awoke and began its slow, merciless crawl through the weekend filings.

At **09:17** a.m. SGT, the bot reached PDF #78214—"EdgeSight Gateway IMDA Type-Approval."

Checksum mismatch.

Metadata showed "**Created with Adobe Acrobat DC 2017**"—problematic, because the original certificate template had been retired in 2014.

The bot auto-generated Query #Q-443581, emailed:

Subject: Possible forged certificate – EdgeSight Gateway

To: *sgcustoms@customs.gov.sg, leon.ng@transastra.sg*

Cc: *mas_alerts@mas.gov.sg*

A silent mouse-click in a server farm fired the first artillery shell of SecuComp's Monday.

1 ▪ Ripple at Changi

05:47 a.m. IST (08:17 a.m. SGT)

Leon Ng wasn't a morning man. His phone's triple-buzz rattled a cup of kopi on his bedside table. He read the email twice, felt his stomach turn. Singapore Customs now demanded physical inspection and engineering test reports within 24 hours—or the entire pallet would be impounded, fines levied, importer black-listed.

Leon speed-dialed Shantanu. No answer. He texted: "**BRO, URGENT, PCC BOT FLAG. NEED REAL CERTS NOW.**"

2 ▪ Monday Stand-Up, Code Red

09:45 a.m. IST – Bengaluru

Weekly stand-up. Engineers huddled around pastries and sarcasm. Shantanu strode in, phone pinging like popcorn. He read Leon's message, felt the pastry cart tilt beneath him.

"Change of agenda," he announced. "We are in DEFCON-2."

Amit frowned. "But Series B docs—"

"Meaningless if Customs seizes cargo."

He tapped the war-room screen: a checklist materialized.

1. Obtain genuine SRRC test report for EdgeSight radio module.
2. Book Singapore lab slot—fast-track, 12-hour turnaround.
3. Fly engineer with sample board to witness test.
4. Draft MAS compliance explanation quoting 'clerical error.'
5. Update investors before rumors leak.

Amit muttered, "Twelve-hour lab turnaround is sci-fi."

"Then write sci-fi into reality," Shantanu snapped.

3 ▪ The Lab that Doesn't Exist

Meera rang four compliance labs. Earliest slot: eight days. Amit called a former Qualcomm colleague, now freelancing RF certifications. The man laughed: "Same-day? You'll need to rent a ghost lane—someone else's booking you quietly slip into."

Price: **USD 25,000** plus no questions asked.

Shantanu okayed it. "Wire from discretionary PR budget."

Meera balked: "That line item's empty."

"Rajat's accrual reversal freed thirty lakhs yesterday. Use it."

Meera's fingers hovered, moral compass spinning, then tapped Proceed.

4 ▪ Devika Draws a Line

12:10 p.m. IST

Devika arrived unannounced, files in hand. Shantanu briefed her, voice low. "This isn't forgery," he insisted. "The hardware passes every spec. We just—accelerate the paperwork."

Devika's gaze was ice. "You doctored a government seal, convinced auditors it was genuine, and traded shares on that basis. Now Customs is on the scent."

Shantanu rubbed temples. "Give me 24 hours. Real cert, clean import, investor call. Then judge."

"I will," Devika said, "But if you slip once, I go public."

She handed him a letter in a sealed envelope—her conditional resignation, datelined tomorrow.

5 ▪ The Courier Dash

15:25 p.m. IST

Amit and junior RF engineer **Shreya Rao** raced to Kempegowda with a single un-encased EdgeSight PCB sealed in ESD pink. Their GoFirst flight to Changi held two diplomatic pouches—coincidentally booked by a defense contractor Shantanu bribed for swap-space.

They rehearsed a cover story: University research prototype, non-commercial, academic exemption. Shreya's nerves jittered; Amit fed her Xanax with airport coffee.

6 ▪ Investor Whispers

17:40 p.m. IST

Boston analyst pinged Varun: Seeing chatter about IMDA hold on SecuComp shipment. True?

Varun forwarded to Shantanu with a single "?"

Shantanu replied:

"Minor paperwork glitch. Engineer on-site. Cert within 24 h. Will update."

He copied Devika. Transparency theatre.

7 ▪ Night in the ISO Tank

22:45 p.m. SGT – Changi

The cargo pallet now occupied an ISO inspection bay—fluorescent lights humming. Leon paced. Customs officer Sergeant Lim eyed the cartons, gloved hands patting labels.

"Certificate inconsistency," Lim said. "Possible fine up to 100,000 SGD."

Leon produced a letter on TransAstra letterhead: clerical template error, genuine test pending. Lim remained stone. "Have engineer here by 10 a.m. with hardware. Else we impound."

8 ▪ Ghost Lane, Real Test

02:10 a.m. SGT (Tuesday)

Amit and Shreya dashed into **WaveCert Labs**, side-door unlocked by a sleepy technician. The "ghost lane" booking name: Electro-Bio Therapeutics. Technician winked, slid the board into an anechoic chamber.

Shreya watched readings stabilize. Radio output at 18 dBm—within IMDA's 20 dBm cap. She exhaled. Technician stamped a fresh PDF, sans watermark, genuine serial number logged in the IMDA portal.

Clock: 04:46 a.m. SGT. They had five hours.

9 ▪ The Broker's Toll

Back in Bengaluru, Meera received a WhatsApp from the ghost-lane fixer: Payment overdue. Release PDF after balance. Amount ballooned to USD 35,000—"overtime surcharge."

Approval chatter quieted; Shantanu made the call. Funds wired. The real certificate dropped into Google Drive.

10 ▪ Customs Showdown

09:52 a.m. SGT

Sergeant Lim studied the new PDF, cross-checked IMDA portal: Status – **APPROVED**. Suspicion lingered, but bureaucracy loves stamped boxes. He unclipped the quarantine seal.

Leon nearly hugged him.

Palettes re-entered free circulation. DHL updated AWB to Released – Out for Delivery. Leon Snap-chatted the moment to Shantanu: **"Green Light, Bro."**

11 ▪ Board Call, Verdict Pending

12:30 p.m. IST (Tuesday)

Board Zoom. Shantanu presented: real cert, customs release, deposit banked. Varun's expression thawed; Rajat smirked; other directors returned nods.

Devika spoke last.

"Compliance restored—for now. But this episode shows systemic ethical lapses." She held up the resignation envelope. Tore it in half, slowly. "One more lapse and the next tear will be the company's."

Shantanu swallowed. "Message received."

12 ▪ The Pale Dawn

04:00 a.m. IST, Wednesday

LaunchPad rooftop again. The city below pulsed with sodium lamps, monorail whine, occasional thunder.

Amit joined him, eyes red. "We cheated death."

"Borrowed time," Shantanu corrected. "We must make numbers real—fast."

He glanced at the horizon, where a thin ribbon of lavender foretold sunrise. Somewhere beyond that glow, Series B wire-rooms hummed, MAS bots scanned, and Devika's conscience stood watch.

He inhaled the tepid, ozone-laced air.

"EdgeSight goes live across fifty plants—or we die honest."

For the first time in weeks, honest sounded less like shackles, more like a north star.

CHAPTER SEVEN

Fifty Plants in Fifty Days

"Make the numbers real—fast."

Those six words became SecuComp's war-cry. Series B papers were with the lawyers, but the money would not hit the bank until Frontier Capital saw live usage, not slide-deck promises. Shantanu set an impossible-sounding target: EdgeSight deployed in fifty industrial sites within fifty calendar days.

The Blitz Map

Amit spread a fresh wall-map in the war-room, sticking coloured pins into it—red for prospects, yellow for dormant pilots, green for existing friendlies. India alone had eighteen lukewarm leads, Southeast Asia ten, and the Gulf fifteen. Natasha Varadarajan, who ran operations like a combat officer, split the conquest into three "lanes." One team would sweep South- and West-Indian auto and cement plants tackling the risk of heavy union rules delay install on the way; another would chase ASEAN food-processing and chemical factories deftly managing the Customs paperwork & language ; the third, led remotely by Leon Ng, would tackle searing-hot Gulf steel yards and logistics hubs. The motto they chanted before every huddle was "five-ten-five": five days to sign, ten to ship, five to activate and invoice.

Sales Shock-Therapy

Pipeline Nair, the deal junkie, launched forty-eight hours of "shock calls." Reps rang every half-warm prospect, dangling a crazy offer: hardware at cost, SaaS fee locked for three years, first sixty days without payment. Factory owners, hungry for efficiency but starved of capex, pounced. In a single frantic shift nine letters of intent landed. Each time the e-mail PDF arrived, the office PA system played a samurai gong—by dawn the corridor sounded like a monastery at war.

Hardware Hurdles

Reality bit back: SecuComp owned only 180 finished gateways, far short of the 450 units the plan required. The Mysuru contract manufacturer was maxed out. Natasha cut a back-alley deal to borrow idle micro-controllers from a defunct wearable start-up; in exchange the founders got a quarter percent of SecuComp stock. Trucks rumbled through monsoon nights, ferrying parts over pot-holed highways while drivers swore at lightning.

Software Scalpel

The cloud backend could barely keep five plants alive without jitter. Amit declared a "code-scalpel" sprint. Vanity analytics were ripped out, the MQTT broker rewritten, and Kubernetes auto-scaling switched on. Junior developers dozed under desks, waking to Grafana dashboards that looked like ICU monitors. Latency fell from four-hundred-plus milliseconds to under a hundred. A round of exhausted claps rippled through the room.

Union Standoff in Tirupati

On day twenty, gateway-installs at Tirupati AutoPress halted when union leader K. Suresh refused safety clearance. Shantanu flew down at dawn, slapped on a hard-hat, and ran a live demo: within minutes the dashboard showed machine idle time shrinking by twelve percent. Overtime wages, Suresh noticed, would jump. He signed. The gong reverberated across Bengaluru.

Sabotage in Surat

Day twenty-seven: at a textile mill in Surat the network collapsed. Logs revealed rogue packets—someone spoofing DHCP to knock gateways offline. Devika traced the source to HelioGrid, a rival IoT vendor. While she drafted a legal threat, Shantanu rang HelioGrid's CEO. "Either the attack patch is live by midnight," he said, "or the packet captures go public with your logo on them." The patch arrived at 22:47; Surat was blue again.

Heatwave in the Gulf

Day thirty-four saw Leon's Dubai crew fighting forty-eight-degree heat. Two gateways overheated and began reboot loops. Shreya pushed a thermal-throttle update from Bengaluru; Amit cut CPU cycles. At sunrise the Dubai logistics hub came back online.

The Numbers Crunch

By day forty-two, the tally read: 392 gateways shipped, thirty-seven sites invoiced, monthly recurring revenue stuck well below target. Varun from Frontier Capital messaged a terse warning: get at least forty-five sites live by day forty-five or the investment committee would "re-examine valuation."

The Triple-Play Weekend

Shantanu announced a "triple-play": three megasites in seventy-two hours. Devika leveraged an old IAS-academy friend to win Haryana AgroChem. Leon flashed a free predictive-maintenance dashboard to Penang Port. Natasha agreed to an on-prem install for Nagpur Smart-Foundry to dodge shaky internet. By Sunday midnight the counter read forty-four.

Crunch-Time Coup

Day forty-nine dawned with the final shipment trapped at Bengaluru airport; officials demanded extra paperwork on lithium batteries. Shantanu marched into Cargo HQ armed with the IMDG code, argued the batteries were under 100 Wh, and discreetly slid an envelope across the desk. The crates cleared.

Installers in Coimbatore and Johor Bahru worked through a steamy night. At twelve minutes past five on day fifty—forty-eight minutes before the deadline—EdgeSight dashboards pinged alive at site number fifty. Natasha, eyes wet, struck the gong herself and nobody turned the volume down.

Investor Euphoria, Founder Exhaustion

Two days later Frontier Capital wired one-sixty crore at a seven-hundred-and-fifty-crore valuation. Tweets hailed SecuComp's "record deployment velocity"—India's answer to Azure-IoT. Television crews arrived; Shantanu, hollow-eyed, spoke of customer obsession and national tech renaissances.

That night, alone in his office, he felt exhaustion crash over him like surf. Forged invoices, ghost-lane certificates, union wrangling, desert heat—all of it pulsed behind his eyelids. Yet, amazingly, the numbers were now real.

He texted Devika: Maybe truth scales faster than lies.

She replied with a single compass emoji.

CHAPTER EIGHT

Shadows Cast Long

The gong's echo had barely faded when consequences began to stalk SecuComp's victory lap—quiet footsteps at first, then pounding boots.

1 ▪ The Email From MAS

Three weeks after the Series B wire, a plain-text e-mail landed in Devika's inbox at 07:12 a.m.

From: surveillance-ops@mas.gov.sg

Subject: Request for Clarifications – EdgeSight Gateway Type-Approval

Singapore's Monetary Authority wanted to examine every correspondence, payment, and test result connected to the overnight certification drama. They gave SecuComp seven working days.

Devika forwarded it to Shantanu with just one line: "Our clock starts now."

2 ▪ Audit Files in Cross-Hairs

Almost in the same hour, India's National Financial Reporting Authority announced a suo-motu review into mid-tier audit firms involved with Series-B-stage tech start-ups. Rajat's shop, Veritas & Co., was on the list.

Rajat phoned Shantanu, voice wobbling. "They want the entire DigiNova work-paper folder. Including e-mails."

Shantanu felt the office walls inch closer. "Give them what's clean. Stall on the rest."

Rajat exhaled like a punctured tyre. "There is no clean."

3 ▪ The Leaked Deck

Frontier Capital's Slack exploded one Tuesday night when an anonymous PDF titled EdgeSight — Unfiltered Risks surfaced. It highlighted forged certificates, ghost customers, and a red-flag memo penned by their own Boston analyst weeks earlier—one Varun had buried.

Frontier's partners smelled blood. Varun's job, and SecuComp's valuation, were suddenly on the table.

4 ▪ Whistle-Blower X

Shantanu guessed instantly who leaked it: Mukund Jha, a freshly laid-off pre-sales engineer who had access to early certification drafts. Mukund's LinkedIn now screamed "Available for new opportunities" and "#EthicalTech." Devika warned Shantanu that Indian whistle-blower protections had real teeth after IL&FS and DHFL fiascos; intimidating Mukund could backfire badly.

5 ▪ Boardroom Fault-Line

Emergency board call. Investor director Gayatri Menon demanded an independent forensic review. Devika endorsed it. Rajat opposed—too expensive, too slow. Shantanu watched allies fracture.

Leon patched in from Dubai, face grey. "Customs here got MAS notice. Gateway batch on my next shipment held at port."

Every angle felt like siege.

6 ▪ A Deal With The Devil

Rajat suggested a desperate gambit: pin everything on "rogue middle-manager actions" and fire two scapegoats—including himself. NFRA might go easier if the board showed swift accountability.

Devika's stare drilled holes. "Scapegoats won't fool regulators. They read e-mail headers too."

But the board was leaning Rajat's way. If Shantanu sacrificed him, perhaps Series B wouldn't down-round.

That night Shantanu opened his laptop to draft Rajat's termination letter. The cursor blinked like a slow, accusing metronome. He couldn't type.

7 ▪ Confession Curveball

Next morning he convened the board in person. Cameras off, phones surrendered. He laid out the entire timeline—fake Swift, ghost lane, bribed cargo clerk. Every ugly stitch. He ended with:

"EdgeSight is saving factories eight percent downtime as we speak. Real value. But we crossed lines to survive. If you want a founder who pretends otherwise, fire me now. If you want to fix it, help me come clean."

Silence, broken only by the hum of the AC.

Devika spoke first. "I'll stay—if the company self-reports to MAS and NFRA by Friday."

Gayatri nodded. "Frontier can still back this, but valuation resets and governance overhaul is non-negotiable."

No one quit the call; no one cheered. It was the sound of a company choosing surgery over morphine.

8 ▪ The Long Week

SecuComp's lawyers drafted a mammoth self-disclosure: every forged document, every bribery receipt, every Slack instruction to "just doctor it." MAS and NFRA accepted the filings, initiated formal probes, but granted provisional leniency under "co-operation credit."

Investors slashed valuation by twenty-five percent yet wired a second tranche, ring-fenced exclusively for compliance upgrades and product scaling. Rajat resigned with a polite LinkedIn note about "new horizons." Shantanu covered his legal fees.

Leon's held shipment cleared after genuine re-testing. Mukund found a job at a rival but never filed a whistle-blower suit—perhaps satisfied that the truth was now public record.

9 ▪ Dawn After Surgery

Two months later, Shantanu stood again on the LaunchPad rooftop. Below him, fifty-plus plants churned real-time data into EdgeSight's dashboards, and a growing handful paid renewal invoices voluntarily. A new Big-4 auditor prowled every ledger entry; the glare felt harsh but strangely freeing.

Devika joined him, holding two mugs of machine coffee. "Still think truth scales faster?"

"Slower," Shantanu admitted, "but it doesn't implode."

She clinked her mug against his. "Welcome to grown-up entrepreneurship."

Down on the street a billboard flashed: **BUILD BOLD, BUILD CLEAN.** For once the slogan felt less like marketing and more like GPS coordinates to a future Shantanu actually wanted to reach.

The shadows were still there—regulators, investors, rivals—but they were finite, defined. And in the scrappy glow of dawn, SecuComp finally looked like a company that could outrun them by simply staying in the light.

CHAPTER NINE

A Market Made of Glass

Six months after SecuComp's tear-stained confession, the company is still standing—but the glass box it lives in now has flood-lights and CCTV. Every quarterly update is livestreamed; one mis-step will send the stock, freshly listed on the SME exchange, into a tail-spin.

The sun had only just climbed above Mysore Road when the first ticker flashed green: SCMP↑12%. Shantanu watched from the buzzing media gallery of the SME exchange, half-numb inside a rented navy blazer. Cameras popped; a news anchor compared SecuComp's debut frenzy to "the next Infosys moment." By 10:15 a.m. the price was up thirty-eight percent, traders on the floor whooping as if the number itself minted rupees.

But beneath the manic bells and confetti lay a hairline crack. Devika, glued to the surveillance dashboard in Bengaluru, spotted a pattern: tiny buy orders firing in perfect sequence—five hundred shares, four hundred, six hundred—always resetting the bid a notch higher, as if an invisible hand were marching the graph upward pixel by pixel. Algorithmic fingerprints, she thought, too tidy for retail chaos. At 10:47 she rang Shantanu. He ducked behind a cardboard Nasdaq-style backdrop.

"*Someone's painting the tape,*" she hissed. "*Wallet IDs trace to Navigator Growth Partners.*"

Shantanu's gut chilled; Navigator was the boutique fund Rajat's cousin ran from a Cayman-registered desk. He recalled a wedding sangeet months earlier, the cousin boasting, "We'll make your listing sizzle, bhai." Shantanu had laughed it off, assuming bluster. Now the laughter soured.

On the trading floor the stock spiked again—forty-two percent—triggering circuit-breaker applause. Reporters shoved mics at him. He recited manufactured humility: "Market sentiment humbles us—we'll keep executing." All the while, Devika's words pounded like a hidden metronome: painting the tape, painting the tape.

By noon the exchange's own algos joined the dots. A compliance officer in a grey Nehru jacket approached, curt nod, whispered: "Sir, we'll need trade data—standard inquiry." The phrase standard inquiry in regulator-speak meant the opposite of standard; it meant storm clouds.

Back at HQ, Gayatri Menon dialled in from Singapore, face tight. "If cousins are juicing your float, MAS leniency is dead on arrival," she warned. Shantanu started to protest, stopped. The board chat exploded—some directors crowing over the price jump, others already gaming indemnity clauses. Rajat, uncharacteristically silent, typed only once: "Looking into it."

The afternoon brought a fresh twist. Telegram groups lit up with conspiracy memes: EdgeScam 2.0 plastered over Shantanu's smiling face, doctored to sprout Pinocchio's nose. Hashtag #DumpSCMP trended by tea-time. Retail punters who had chased the morning rally now stampeded for exits, and the price yo-yoed like a kite in cross-winds.

At 3:25 p.m., fifteen minutes before closing bell, Devika burst into Shantanu's glass cubicle. "Navigator wallets just dumped every share—they're out." Price sank ten percent in three ticks. The cheers outside died, replaced by the insect hum of TV crews rewriting headlines from Rocket Listing to Roller-Coaster Debut.

After the bell, the exchange summoned management for a Monday-morning hearing. Rajat's cousin went dark, phone off, offices "on annual audit." Shantanu's triumph morphed into dread as quickly as the ticker had flipped digits. Standing before the blank CCTV monitor that governed the trading hall, he saw his reflection ghosted on the glass—celebrity one moment, suspect the next, both images transparent to those who knew where to look.

The market had welcomed SecuComp, yes, but on terms as brittle as the glass panes that surrounded him: beautiful until pressure found a fault line. And somewhere in that glittering fracture, Shantanu realised, lay the true opening price of integrity—not set by exuberant traders, but by how fast a founder owned the mess before the mess owned him

CHAPTER TEN

Acquisition Smells Too Sweet

The Monday after the listing fiasco, Shantanu should have been buried in compliance binders—but temptation knows perfect timing. His phone buzzed with a message from Arjun Salvi, venture banker and weekend golf buddy:

PixeLore is in play—20 PhDs, breakthrough anomaly AI, quick close possible.

Asking ₹60 crore, half cash, half stock. AWS circling.

Meet noon?

Shantanu forwarded the teaser to CTO Amit, COO Natasha, and Devika with a single line: "**Could this plug our analytics gap overnight?**" Amit replied with a shrug emoji; Devika sent a red-flag GIF; Natasha typed, "Due-diligence first."

The Pitch

At noon, Arjun swept into SecuComp's glass boardroom carrying a leather folio and his trademark evangelical grin. Two young founders from PixeLore—sleepless eyes, black t-shirts—clicked through a sizzle deck: self-healing models, zero false positives, slides peppered with Fortune 500 pilots and a glowing Gartner quote.

Shantanu felt the old adrenaline: **Buy them before a giant does**. Rajat, still licking wounds from the listing probe, applauded the "transformative synergy." Director **Samir Kothari** leaned back, calling it a "table-stakes acqui-hire." Only Gayatri and Devika stayed poker-faced.

Amit asked for model benchmarks; the founders said NDAs forbade sharing raw metrics. Natasha inquired about customer contracts; they admitted the pilots were still "letter-of-intent stage." Arjun waved it off:

"Early traction—same as you guys once."

The room divided—dreamers versus drillers—until Dr Mira Shekhar dialled in late. She listened, silent, then requested one document: "The valuation memo." Arjun slid over two pages of banker jargon, rich on comparables, thin on revenue. Mira ended the call with three words: "Smells like perfume."

Peeling the Perfume

Natasha dispatched her finance lieutenant, Kavya, for a "stress-diligence." Within forty-eight hours they found:

- The much-lauded AI code had a 90-percent overlap with an MIT open-source library.
- PixeLore's "20 PhDs" were mostly masters' interns on three-month stipends.
- One of the Fortune-500 logos was, in fact, a pilot proposal—but the customer had gone with AWS.

Amit ran the code on EdgeSight's test bed: acceptable precision, but nothing revolutionary. Cost to build in-house? Roughly one-tenth the asking price.

Meanwhile Devika back-channelled a Gartner analyst; the glowing quote came from a generic blog, not official research. Samir accused her of "paralysis by analysis." She fired back: "Analysis is how we avoid prison." The board Slack went radioactive.

The Poker Showdown

Wednesday evening, Arjun pushed for term-sheet signing. "AWS has a verbal at seventy crore," he insisted. Gayatri requested the name of AWS's corporate dev lead; Arjun dodged. Mira invoked the new Noise-Gate rule: two independent valuations or no vote. Samir lobbied to waive it—"We'll lose the deal!"

At 9 p.m., Shantanu gathered his inner circle—Gayatri, Mira, Devika, Amit, Natasha. The projector showed two paths:

- Sign now: Silence critics, headline-grab, spend precious cash.
- Walk away: Risk press calling them timid, but keep powder dry.

Shantanu stared at the term-sheet, remembering the forged certificates, the listing probe, the tape-painting cousin. One more corner-cut could tip the regulators from lenient to lethal.

He slid the document back across the table. "We build, we don't bluff."

Mira's half-smile said about time. Gayatri nodded, relief visible. Amit exhaled. Devika tapped a phrase into Slack: "**Deal declined—home-brew begins**." Samir sighed theatrically, but the vote was 4–2. The Noise-Gate held.

Fallout

Arjun's follow-up e-mail dripped with wounded pride. Tech blogs ran "SecuComp passes on AI gem—hubris?" AWS announced no such acquisition; the rumour evaporated. Three weeks later PixeLore slashed staff and dropped price to ₹18 crore; still no takers.

Inside SecuComp, Amit's skunk-works cloned the same anomaly engine in six sprints. Cost: ₹5.7 crore, all in. Accuracy beat PixeLore's demo by twelve points.

Shantanu sent a company-wide note:

"We just proved something: urgency without diligence is vanity.
The market can hype; we'll verify."

The message landed harder than any gong ever had. Across the open floor, engineers stuck fresh posters: **BUILD • VERIFY • SLEEP WELL.**

And somewhere between the shattered glamour of an easy buy and the grind of writing clean code, SecuComp found a new muscle: the discipline to say **No**—loudly, publicly, unashamed—before a Yes could mutate into scandal.

CHAPTER ELEVEN

Paper Tigers in the C-Suite

The ink on the rejected PixeLore term sheet was barely dry when SecuComp's spotlight swung inward, illuminating its own high-paid mirages.

The Sizzle Gurus

Rohit "ROI" Mehta – Senior VP, Growth Strategy. MBA wall lined with framed keynote passes, fluent in acronyms, allergic to Jira.

Sneha "Synergy" Bhandari – Senior VP, Platform Alliances. Former McKinsey partner, legendary for TED-style monologues that began with Greek myths and ended with revenue forecasts no analyst could trace.

Together they sold the board on **EdgeSight Social**—a gamified dashboard that would "turn factory shop-floors into collaborative communities." Rohit promised pilot launch in six months, incremental ARR of ₹50 crore in year one. Budget approved: ₹4 crore.

Eight months passed. Conference-room walls filled with journey maps and mood boards, but no code made it to staging. Whenever Amit pressed for builds, Rohit waved "design thinking sprints"; Sneha cited "partner alignment phases."

The Day of Screenshots

Natasha, now armed with Mira's Noise-Gate authority, scheduled a "live demo" for the next board meeting. Rohit arrived sleek in charcoal suit, Sneha in trademark silk scarf. They plugged in a laptop; a dazzling UI appeared—avatars, leaderboards, real-time emojis floating over machine metrics.

Amit squinted, opened dev tools: the app called images from /assets/ mock/; every click dead-ended in coming-soon.html. He leaned to Shantanu and whispered, "Pure Figma, zero backend."

Devika asked gently, "Could we log in as a supervisor?" Rohit stammered about "beta credentials." Mira's eyes narrowed. Gayatri requested Git commit logs; Sneha replied that code lived in "distributed innovation pods." Translation: nowhere.

Empty Repositories Exposed

Natasha unleashed Kavya again. Three days of audit revealed:

- Spend: ₹3.78 crore—70% on freelancers, UI agencies, motivational off-sites.
- GitHub repo: four commits—two README files, one license, one GIF.
- Claimed partner pilots: nonexistent; the cited companies denied knowledge.

Kavya's report hit the board Slack at 1:12 a.m. title line—**"EdgeSight Social = VaporSight."**

Confrontation

An emergency board sits. Rohit opens with a pre-emptive flourish: "Innovation isn't linear—ask Steve Jobs." Mira interjects, "Jobs shipped." Sneha cites market headwinds; Gayatri shows the repo on screen—blank. Samir tries to pivot blame toward "resource constraints"; Devika counters with budget burn chart bleeding red.

Shantanu feels an old instinct to shield his hires—then pictures the glass box market, the regulators, the congress of whistle-blowers circling LinkedIn like hawks. He turns to Rohit and Sneha.

"Deliverables in sixty days or we reassign the project and review your roles."

Sneha bristles. "That's not how agile creativity works." Mira replies, "No, that's how fiduciary duty works."

Vote: immediate termination of EdgeSight Social, redeploy unspent budget to actual customer requested features. Rohit and Sneha exit with curated LinkedIn posts about "pursuing disruptive horizons." Inside SecuComp, a spontaneous Slack emoji storm of party confetti erupts.

Lessons Pinned to the Wall

Poster added beside ***BUILD • VERIFY • SLEEP WELL***

TALK LESS – SHIP MORE

PowerPoint is cheap; production logs are truth.

A week later, an engineer previously buried under Rohit's bureaucracy ships a maintenance-alert widget customers had requested for months.

Downtime at three pilot plants drops 5%. Actual ARR climbs   ₹
1.8 crore—small, real, early.

Shantanu walks the floor, hearing keyboards not slogans. For the first time since the IPO circus, the office hum resembles an engine tuned for distance, not fireworks.

CHAPTER TWELVE

Stock-Manipulation Storm

The lull after the C-suite purge lasted barely a fortnight before thunderheads gathered over SecuComp's ticker once more.

A Knock at Dawn

7:06 a.m., mid-week. Two officials from the exchange's Surveillance & Enforcement Division waited in reception, crisp in grey Nehru jackets. They presented Shantanu with formal summonses for trading records, phone logs, and e-mails dated the week of SecuComp's listing.

Their tone was courteous; the sub-text lethal: "**Possible co-ordinated manipulation under SEBI Section 12A.**"

Deadline: five working days.

Chat-Log Grenades

Compliance chief Devika pulled phone metadata first. Pattern emerged: Rajat's cousin **Aakash Mehra** exchanged 47 WhatsApp messages with director Samir Kothari between 8 a.m. and 3 p.m. on listing day—precisely when those suspicious bursts of buy-and-dump trades hit the tape.

Gayatri, chair of audit, convened an emergency committee. Samir dialled in from Goa, voice breezy: "Family office managers handle allocations; I was merely congratulating Aakash." Devika screenshared emoji-laden chats:

- **Aakash**: "Pump set, bro—watch the spike!"
- **Samir**: "Haha, let's make fireworks. ??"

Silence settled over the Zoom. Even the AC hum seemed accusatory.

The Conflict Disclosure

Dr Mira Shekhar invoked Clause 49 of the Listing Agreement: directors must disclose related-party dealings immediately or face disqualification. Samir protested, "Those were personal messages, not instructions." Mira countered: "Intent is immaterial; perception rules public markets."

The board voted 5–1 to suspend Samir from all committees pending investigation. He logged off without farewell. Within an hour, media broke "SEC UCOMP DIRECTOR SUSPENDED IN TAPE-RIGGING PROBE." Share price sagged 12 percent. Telegram hysteria roared back to life.

Aakash Goes Dark

Exchange officers hunted Aakash's Cayman shell, but the fund's servers sat behind offshore secrecy. Shantanu's lawyer advised distancing—publicly. Devika drafted a press release:

"SecuComp is fully co-operating with regulators.
No director or officer authorised any stock-price action."

She posted it before legal could water it down. Investors grumbled; transparency, again, was the only anaesthetic.

The Independent Audit

Under MAS leniency terms, SecuComp was already subject to quarterly forensic reviews. Gayatri fast-tracked the next audit, empowering Big-4 firm Ashworth & Young to trace every listing-day communication. For two sleepless weeks, analysts scraped Slack, sifted call logs, reconstructed trade ledgers.

Findings:

- Shantanu had zero contact with Aakash pre-listing.
- Rajat's last WhatsApp was months earlier—harmless memes.
- Samir's messages, while damning in tone, lacked explicit trade direction.

Recommendation: censure Samir, ban related-party trades for all insiders six months pre–post listing, strengthen messaging archives.

SEBI's Verdict (Interim)

Regulator issued an interim order:

- Aakash Mehra – barred from markets for one year, pending final adjudication.
- Navigator Growth Partners – assets frozen equivalent to trading gains.
- Samir Kothari – prohibited from board positions in listed firms for six months; heavy monetary penalty mooted after hearing.

Crucially, no charges against SecuComp or Shantanu. The market exhaled; stock clawed back half its drop.

Aftermath Inside the Glass Box

Samir's office nameplate vanished overnight. In its place a sticky note: **"Noise-Gate Wins Again."** Staff snapped photos; Twitter turned it into a governance meme.

Shantanu gathered employees in the town-hall space once used for flashy launch parties. No stage lights, just plain fluorescents.

"We have now survived forged certificates, a glamour-deal trap, vapor-ware executives, and a boardroom conflict that could have sunk us.
Each disaster taught us the same lesson: daylight hurts, but darkness kills.
We choose daylight—every time."

Applause began tentative, then rolled like distant monsoon thunder. In that clap of hands lay a collective vow: SecuComp would rather bleed in transparency than drown in scandal.

Forward Traction

- Governance charter amended: all board chats auto-archived, real-time compliance alerts on any insider trade.
- Investor calls rescheduled as open webinars—analysts, regulators, employees welcome.
- Share price stabilised in a narrow, honest band—no more fireworks, no cliff-dives.

The market remained a glass box. But every new pane installed—policies, audits, disclosures—made the structure less brittle, more like tempered glass that bends before it breaks.

And somewhere outside, would-be manipulators marked SecuComp off their soft-target lists. A company once notorious for shortcuts was becoming infamous for something rarer: being too hard to corrupt.

CHAPTER THIRTEEN

Patriot Act Decision – Revisited

Barely a month after the tape-rigging storm subsided, New Delhi lobbed its own thunderbolt: a draft **Critical Data Localisation Bill,** nicknamed "The Patriot Act of the East." Clause 7(b) declared that "all sensor or telemetry data generated by core manufacturing in Indian territory must be processed and stored on servers physically located within India." Violations carried fines of up to ₹50 crore and potential criminal liability for "controlling founders."

Flashpoint

EdgeSight's architecture streamed terabytes nightly through Singapore and Frankfurt. Re-wiring to India-only zones meant new racks, sovereign-cloud contracts, doubled latency, and a brutal hit to margin. Rival corporates immediately pounced- Reliance launched ads proclaiming "Proudly 100 % Swadeshi Cloud." VCs whispered that SecuComp's cost base had just imploded.

The War-Room

Shantanu convened the full board in a windowless strategy bunker that still smelled of fresh paint from the last crisis. Three options filled the whiteboard:

- **Mirror Everything in India** – clean, lawful, cripplingly expensive.
- **Edge-Anonymise, Then Export** – cheaper, legally gray, PR minefield.
- **Lobby for a Carve-Out** – uncertain, slow, reeks of back-room politics.

In earlier days, this debate would have been a cacophony of egos. Not now.

- **Gayatri Menon** ran cost projections—mirroring would slash EBITDA by nine points.
- Amit warned latency might erode predictive accuracy.
- Natasha showed customer survey heat-maps—trust dipped whenever compliance looked fuzzy.
- **Dr Mira Shekhar** spoke last: "Regulators remember faces. After Satyam, DHFL, Samir's cousin-do we want our face in question-hour?"

No one did.

Samir's seat sat empty, a spectral reminder of shortcuts past.

The Conscience Vote

The board had adopted electronic roll-call voting—results projected instantly for all employees watching the internal livestream.

Gayatri Menon – Aye (Option 1)

Devika Rao – Aye

Amit Paranjpe – Aye

Natasha Singh – Aye

Dr Mira Shekhar – Aye

Rajat Deshpande – Aye (surprising even himself)

Vacant Seat – —

Result: 6 – 0. Unanimous.

The livestream chat erupted in thumbs-up emojis. One line stood out: "Margin recovers; integrity doesn't. Proud to build here."

BharatVault, Version 2

Engineers christened the new cluster **BharatVault** and attacked the rebuild like a moon-shot. Shreya wrote a time-series compressor that shrank storage needs by 40% Kavya negotiated volume discounts with three Indian cloud vendors by playing them against each other on a public Slack channel regulators could witness. Every sprint review was livestreamed; roadblocks were logged in Jira and on a public Confluence page.

Forty-three days in, SEBI officials performed a surprise walk-through. They found sleepless

coders, transparent dashboards, and—crucially—**no sidebooks.**

Launch Day

Day 110. Factory managers, union reps, and even a junior commerce-ministry officer crowded into the gleaming new NOC. A "data-origin" display shaped like the Indian map pulsed green as packets flowed exclusively between domestic zones. When the first predictive alert fired and a plant in Surat averted a conveyor breakdown live on screen, applause rolled like factory drums.

Markets React

Analysts had braced for margin collapse. Instead, cost-savings from Shreya's compression and

Kavya's vendor war pared the EBITDA hit to four points—recoverable within two quarters. Brokerage notes labeled SecuComp **"compliance-ready"** and upgraded the stock. The price ticked up a quiet, honest 6%.

Legacy

Dr Mira pinned a new maxim next to the BUILD and TALK LESS posters:

LAW BEFORE LORE

Folklore says bend rules;
longevity says write new ones.

Shantanu, reading it during a rare calm evening, realised something profound: each crisis had carved away a layer of bravado, leaving a company that was humbler, costlier to run—but finally antifragile. The glass box had become tempered glass—still transparent, but able to take a hit without shattering.

He messaged Devika a single word: "**Forward.**"

She replied with the compass emoji and, for the first time, a small white star.

CHAPTER FOURTEEN

Re-Wiring the Cloud

A green status map didn't end the battle; it only changed the terrain. Moving every byte of EdgeSight telemetry inside India meant swapping decades-hardened global tooling for an eclectic mix of desi stacks, each with its own quirks and unpatched ghosts.

"Welcome to Jugaad-Ops"

Amit christened the migration sprint Project Jugaad-Ops—equal parts innovation and duct tape. Bengaluru's Dev floor looked like a hardware flea market: new 100-gig routers stacked beside dusty rack mounts scavenged from a bankrupt crypto-mine in Noida. Engineers wore "LAW BEFORE LORE" tees; caffeine flowed like cooling fluid.

Shreya's time-series compressor slashed disk burn, but the real choke point was compute. Domestic clouds throttled burst capacity during India's nightly power-grid oscillations. Predictive models stuttered at 2 a.m., right when factories spun up graveyard shifts.

Natasha ran nightly fire-drills: when latency spiked, teams had ten minutes to fail over to backup zones—or buy samosas for everyone. Weight gain became a compliance metric.

The Ghost of Mukund Jha

Mid-migration, Devika's SIEM console spat an alert: an ancient admin token pinged a staging box—credentials belonging to Mukund Jha, the ex-ops whistle-blower. His account should have died two years earlier.

Amit traced the attempt to a disposable VPS in Belarus. Someone was probing the new walls before the cement dried.

They purged every legacy credential, spun an air-gap staging environment, and added an "I Am Alive" heartbeat for each micro-service—miss three beats, auto-isolate, kill token. Engineers dubbed it the SpectreFence.

Boardroom Thunder—Again

At the next governance call, cost overruns loomed—	₹12 crore above budget. Investors grumbled about "over-engineering." Gayatri flashed latency graphs: old infra 180 ms, BharatVault 95 ms post-SpectreFence. She closed with a single slide: Fine for Non-Compliance:	₹50 crore + Jail.

Silence. Budget approved.

Dr Mira added a note to the minutes: "Pay today or pay prosecutors tomorrow."

Midnight Zero-Day

Day 72. Log4Shell-style zero-day hits a popular desi logging library that BharatVault relies on. Patches nonexistent. At 01:13, SOC dashboards flare crimson. Amit orders a code gray. Services down-shift into read-only "safe lake" mode; factories receive SMS alerts to switch manual.

In Surat, union leader Suresh awakens maintenance crews before a conveyor jam becomes a fireball. One hour later, Shreya hot-patches the vulnerable jar, rebuilds images. Total downtime: 62 minutes; no injuries, no fines.

Social media explodes with praise instead of anger. #BharatVault trended higher than cricket hashtags for the first time.

The Ledger of Wins

Latency: down 47%.

Predictive accuracy: +6%.

Compliance scorecard: 100% green on SEBI's new real-time audit API.

Customer churn: negative—two ex-clients returned, citing "bullet-proof compliance."

Anand, a cynical senior engineer, updated the office posters one last time:

BUILD • VERIFY • SLEEP WELL

TALK LESS – SHIP MORE

LAW BEFORE LORE

WIN BY PATCHING FASTER THAN THEY CAN EXPLOIT

Shantanu walked the floor at dawn, reading each line. The glass walls reflected a company no longer posturing, simply operating—faster, cleaner, harder to hack.

Foreshadow: SpectreFox Watches

Unbeknownst to them, an anonymous darknet forum posted a bounty: "Break BharatVault, prove swadeshi cloud is sieve. 50 BTC." The signature:

SpectreFox.

SecuComp's new fortress invited a bigger siege. But for the first time, the defenders felt ready—and the board, once a rubber-stamp chorus, now stood as armoured sentries.

CHAPTER FIFTEEN

Customers Day

SecuComp called it an Open Ops House; the press called it judgment day. One hundred guests—plant managers in oil-smudged overalls, union heads in starched khadi, mid-level regulators clutching tablets, and two dozen skeptics from tech media—filed through the glass doors that once hid forged invoices.

Factory-Floor First Impressions

They expected polished demos; instead, Amit walked them straight into the war-room. Live Grafana boards pulsed with machine vitals from Pune, Chennai, and Vizag. A conveyor bearing in Gujarat spiked yellow; an alert projected both the raw sensor waveform and BharatVault packet trace.
Suresh, the Surat union leader, nudged a journalist: "That spike nearly torched my guys last month. They iced it in five minutes." Cameras clicked; skeptics scribbled.

Transparency Theatre

Natasha handed visitors NFC badges that opened read-only views of SecuComp's real Jira, Confluence, and the NFRA audit dashboard. Nothing staged. Kavya even displayed procurement contracts—vendors, rates, and the bidding history that squeezed cost down 22%. One regulator whispered, "Never seen this level of disclosure outside court subpoenas."

The Compass Wall

In the atrium, a giant LED compass glowed. Each degree marked a crisis: forged certificates (18°), PixeLore scam (103°), VaporSight purge (147°), Tape-Rigging probe (193°), BharatVault build (270°). At 360° a star lit up: the moment the localisation cluster went live and remained breach-free for 90 days.

Devika explained: "Every time we face true north—truth, not convenience—the compass completes a circle. Miss north, we spin forever."

Factory managers photographed it like a pilgrimage relic.

Union Seal of Approval

During Q&A, a reporter lobbed the inevitable grenade: "Your EBITDA fell; was honesty worth it?"

Suresh took the mic before Shantanu could.

"I saw lives nearly lost to hidden shortcuts. Their new rules stopped that. Profit can grow again; dead workers can't."

Applause thundered, drowning follow-up questions.

A Surprise Ally

Mid-tour, SEBI's junior officer received a ping—her chief had joined the livestream, impressed. He posted in chat: "Textbook compliance-as-a-service. Other vendors should benchmark this." Investors watching remote feeds screen-grabbed the comment; WhatsApp analyst groups buzzed.

Closing Bell

At 4 p.m. Shantanu stepped onto a modest dais—no fireworks, just white-board slides.

"We promised daylight over shortcuts. Today daylight promised us growth that regulators, unions, and customers can trust. We're slower than hype but faster than fear. Welcome to profit at the speed of trust."

When the guests left, a literal rainbow arced over Bengaluru's evening haze—someone took it as divine IPO-do-over marketing, but Shantanu just smiled and went back to the incident queue.

Metrics Next Morning

- New pipeline RFPs: +17% overnight.
- Churn probability score: falls to an all-time low 0.8%.
- Media sentiment index: flips from −35 to +22.
- Share price: steady—no spike, no slide, just an honest uptick.

The Shadow Post

At midnight, SpectreFox dropped a dark-web post: "Glass looks strong; every fortress has a sewer." The bounty doubled. But inside SecuComp, engineers were already patching a minor credential leak found during the tour—before SpectreFox could.

The glass box remained under siege, but the audience now included allies who would shout if cracks appeared. Daylight had become armor.

Ransomware Eclipse

The rainbow of Customer Day had barely faded when midnight alarms howled like air-raid sirens.

00:03 – The Blackout

Every BharatVault dashboard snapped to crimson. Packet loss spiked to 100 % across Zone-C—home to half of SecuComp's predictive workloads. A single message scrawled itself on Grafana in looping ASCII:

SPECTREFOX GRANTS YOU DARKNESS.

PAY 50 BTC OR WATCH YOUR NORTH STAR DIE.

Files on Zone-C nodes renamed to *.eclipse; encryption keys unknown. The clock beneath the ransom note bled down from **96 h 00 m.**

00:07 – Code Grey+

Amit invoked Code Grey+—full lockdown plus regulatory self-report within one hour. Devika rang SEBI's night line while sending an automated breach disclosure to every customer. No excuses, no PR glaze—Subject: *Immediate Security Incident – Mitigation Underway.*

Factory lines in Surat, Pune, and Vizag flicked to manual. Months of trust would evaporate if production halted at dawn.

00:22 – The Ghost Token Resurfaces

Shreya traced the intrusion path: SpectreFox exploited **CVE-84912**, a zero-day in the desi cloud's metadata API, then rode an obsolete admin token—Mukund Jha's ghost again—to escalate across Zone-C. It was the sewer SpectreFox had promised.

Amit cursed, "We're all-in on localisation, and the weakest link is the local vendor's code." But there was a sliver of hope—Zone-C's backups replicated every six hours to an isolated safe-lake Shreya had insisted on after Log4Shell.

Latest clean snapshot: **T-4 h 17 m.**

01:10 – Board on the Bridge

Shantanu pushed an emergency Zoom to all directors. Faces appeared in night-lamps and car interiors. Gayatri's voice was steel: "Plan?"

Amit: *"Cut Zone-C, restore from safe-lake, patch CVE, rotate all tokens. Downtime two hours if luck holds."*

Natasha: "Factories survive manual for three—but regulators must watch us fight."

Dr Mira: *"Livestream the incident room to SEBI and unions. They'll forgive outage, not secrecy."*

Unanimous nods. No grandstanding. Shantanu felt déjà vu—except this time the board was weapon, not weakness.

01:35 – Livestream War-Room

A secure YouTube link went out: War-Room Live – SpectreFox Eclipse. 1,200 viewers ballooned to 20,000: customers, analysts, a CNBC anchor, even rival CTOs.

They watched Shreya's terminal cascade commands, Kavya negotiate burst compute from a rival cloud, Amit's eyes scanning logs like Morse code. Each success posted as a green tick; each failure in red with ETA. No marketing filter.

In chat, union leader Suresh typed: *"We stand by ops crew—keep belts running safe."* Likes exploded.

02:47 – The Turn of the Tide

Patch compiled. Safe-lake image verified. Shreya executed restore_zone_c --snap 04:16 --parallel 20. Progress bar crawled; viewers held breath. At 86%, SpectreFox injected a final taunt: "Restore this, heroes." A second payload tried to hijack Kubernetes API—but Devika's SpectreFence heartbeat auto-isolated the node. Silence, then applause in the chat.

03:08 – Restore hit 100%. Zone-C heartbeat green. Total blackout: 3 h 05 m—inside promised SLA.

04:20 – Dawn Status

Surat conveyor hum resumed; Pune robots re-synced. Zero injuries, zero missed exports. Shreya killed the ransom clock at 92 h 40 m left, posting a GIF of Gandalf facing the Balrog: "YOU SHALL NOT PASS."

08:00 – Global Ripples

- Tech press headlined: **"Transparency Beats Ransom—SecuComp Fights Hack Live."**
- Share price dipped 4% at open, recovered by lunchtime.
- SEBI tweeted rare praise: "Incident response exemplary; other issuers take note."
- Rival CTOs requested joint working group on desi-cloud security.

SpectreFox's darknet bounty thread went silent. Rumour said the attacker lost face—and potential bidders—when thousands witnessed his defeat in real time.

After-Action Etching

On the Compass Wall, engineers etched a new mark at 315°: **Ransomware Eclipse – Fought in Daylight**. Beneath it, a fresh maxim appeared:

SHADOWS FEAR OPEN ROOMS

Broadcast the battle, and the enemy's power dims.

Epilogue to Eclipse

Shantanu closed his first-light journal entry:

"We asked if daylight could be armor.

Tonight it became our sword."

The glass box, scarred but unbroken, now reflected not just transparency but resilience forged in the furnace of public scrutiny. SpectreFox might strike again; others surely would. Yet every assault carved deeper trust in a market that finally understood: SecuComp's true product was integrity operationalised at scale.

CHAPTER SEVENTEEN

Justice Flight

The ransomware dust had barely settled when subpoenas crossed oceans.

Aakash's Vanishing Act

Cayman authorities, prodded by SEBI and India's Enforcement Directorate, unsealed Navigator Growth Partners' shell records. They found wire trails plunging through Belize, Luxembourg, finally to a Hong Kong charter-jet operator. Aakash Mehra had purchased a one-way Gulfstream hop the same morning SecuComp livestreamed its SpectreFox victory—destination: Monaco, beyond India's extradition reach.

Gayatri forwarded the dossier to the board with one line: "Flight risk confirmed."

The Extradition Gambit

India's Ministry of Finance sensed a trophy case. They launched Operation Justice Flight: a coalition of ED officers, SEBI forensic accountants, and an Interpol liaison set on freezing every asset Aakash touched.

Shantanu watched warily; any misstep might splash back on SecuComp. Devika compiled a Zero-Ties Certificate—timestamped comms, HR records, audit memos—proving the company severed all links the moment tape-rigging surfaced. She mailed it to regulators before they asked.

Samir in the Dock

Meanwhile, suspended director Samir Kothari faced SEBI's adjudication bench. Livestreamed hearings became instant corporate soap opera. Prosecutors displayed his "Pump set, bro" emojis; Samir's counsel blamed "light-hearted banter." Dr Mira served as expert witness, dismantling that defense with Clause 49 precedent.

Verdict:

Market-ban: 5 years

Penalty: ₹8 crore

Mandatory governance training before any future board seat

Media hailed it as the toughest punishment for a non-executive insider since the Satyam era.

A Surprise Ally on the Stand

During cross-examination, Mira quoted SecuComp's Compass Wall maxims. Reporters ate it up—governance poetry. SEBI chair publicly thanked SecuComp for "setting the gold standard in self-disclosure." For once, a company's name shone in a fraud trial not as culprit but as compass.

The Monaco Maneuver

Interpol finally traced Aakash's yacht, Glint Voyager, berthed in Port Hercule. But Monaco required airtight evidence to seize assets. Indian agencies lacked the digital forensics tying Navigator's illicit profits directly to market manipulation.

Enter SecuComp's transparency trove. Gayatri authorised release of sanitized, hash-verified trading-day logs. Natasha and Devika packaged them with a cryptographic chain-of-custody. Within days, Monaco's financial crimes bureau froze €9 million across Aakash's accounts.

Aakash's lawyer shrieked about "corporate vendetta"; French media instead framed it as "La tech indienne expose un fraudeur global."

Ramifications at 35,000 Feet

News of the freeze travelled faster than jets. Family offices from Dubai to Singapore began quietly querying their portfolio companies: "Show us your Compass Wall equivalents." A governance meme had crossed borders, powered by SecuComp's brutal honesty.

VC firm Coastal Rise circulated an LP letter:

"Our new term-sheets adopt the SecuComp Clause—mandatory public incident streams for any breach or regulatory probe."

What began as crisis choreography became policy.

Boardroom Reflection

Back in Bengaluru, Shantanu addressed a smaller, leaner board—Samir's seat still empty, now deliberately left vacant as memorial. He summarised:

Tape-rigging scandal closing with convictions

Ransomware defeat boosting trust metrics

Customer pipeline at record high

Market steady, regulators citing them as model

Then he posed a question: "We turned transparency into a shield and sword. How do we keep edge without turning paranoid?"

Dr Mira replied, "By remembering the glass box doesn't guard itself; we polish it daily or let dust become disguise."

Gayatri proposed a quarterly Ethics Hackathon—invite white-hat hackers, auditors, even rival CTOs to hunt flaws live for prize money. Unanimous vote: Aye.

Compass Completes a Second Circle

On the Compass Wall, engineers lit a new star at 0°—Justice Flight Intercepted—closing a second full revolution since forged certificates. Two circles, one above the other, formed an infinity symbol: integrity is never a single lap; it loops, forever.

Below, a final maxim for this turn:

TRANSPARENCY IS VELOCITY

The clearer we fly, the faster we outrun fraud.

Shantanu stood before the luminous eight, feeling the company nose upward. SpectreFox might sharpen claws, regulators might toughen rules, markets might wobble—but SecuComp had found an engine powered by glass and truth, and it was gaining altitude with every crisis faced head-on.

CHAPTER EIGHTEEN

Ethics Hackathon

A rainy Friday in Bengaluru. Neon reflections shimmered on the driveway as a rag-tag procession of laptops, hoodies, blazers and briefcases funneled into SecuComp HQ. Banners read "Break Us — Win ₹1 Crore" and "All Logs Public. All Eyes Welcome."

Check-In: Badges of Intent

White hats clipped visitor tags that glowed green.

Auditors & regulators sported blue.

Rival CTOs wore yellow—competitive neutrality.

Media donned red, the colour of recording lights.

A final category—grey—received black badges labelled Observer. One grey-badge, a soft-spoken woman with silver piercings, signed "SpectreFox?" in the pseudonym field. The receptionist merely smiled: rules allowed aliases.

Opening Salvo

Shantanu took no stage—he stood among folding chairs. "You already know our scars," he began, motioning to the Compass Wall livestreamed overhead. "Your mission: exploit any weakness we've missed. If you succeed, you get one crore and your name on that wall. If you fail, you still get applause—and samosas." Laughter thawed tension.

The Arena

- Target 1: BharatVault sandbox, seeded with synthetic factory data.
- Target 2: Live incident-stream pipeline (the very camera feed watchers were viewing).
- Target 3: Governance Slack clone with redacted but real decision graphs.

Everything except production databases was in play. The only forbidden act: endangering a real worker.

Amit triggered the countdown: 24 hours.

First Blood – The CORS Gambit

At 01 h 27 m, Team NullPointers exploited a permissive CORS header on a debug sub-domain, stealing a session cookie. They posted the PoC in the public Discord; Devika's team patched in 23 minutes, awarding ₹5 lakh bounty. Applause in cafeteria; leaderboard lit up.

The Grey-Badge Shadow

Silver-piercing grey-badge—codename Argent—worked alone, no chatter. She probed the SpectreFence heartbeat API, fuzzing payload sizes. Kavya monitored her IP hops; nothing malicious yet, just mapping.

03 h 50 m: Argent DM'd Amit through the hackathon chat: "Heartbeat drops three beats if packet is exactly 65,535 bytes with crafted CRC. Opens 30-second blind spot." Proof attached. It was the first credible bypass of SpectreFence.

Amit's eyes widened. Instead of patching silently, he asked Argent to present on stage. She agreed on one condition: "Stream it live." Terms accepted.

Live Dissection

Under camera glare, Argent explained how integer-overflow in vendor NIC firmware caused an undetected reset, letting an attacker race a rogue command. Engineers patched firmware and doubled heartbeat frequency; blind spot shrank to 5 seconds. Audience cheered; Argent's name—real or not—hit the Compass Wall.

Bounty raised to ₹30 lakh; half donated by Argent to a public bug-bounty foundation. Hashtag #HackWithLight trended.

Midnight Merge-Fest

By 02 a.m. the repo showed 142 merged pull requests—patches, logging tweaks, even UI dark-mode built by a designer from a rival firm "for eye comfort while hacking." The event morphed into communal refactorathon.

SEBI's on-site officer tweeted:

"Watching competitors fortify a listed company in real time. Future of regulation = open glass boxes."

The Last Hour – SpectreFox Signal?

At 23 h 10 m, logs flagged a surge of anomaly traffic from TOR nodes hammering the restored heartbeat endpoint. Someone tried Argent's exploit pre-patch. SpectreFence v2 held. Devika tagged it POSSIBLE SPECTREFOX PROBE on the public dashboard. Thousands watched the attack flatten against fresh code; chat erupted in digital fist-bumps.

Closing Bell

Timer hit zero. Scoreboard:

Critical vulns found & fixed: 7

Moderate issues: 22

Cosmetic / UX suggestions merged: 31

Service interruptions: 0

Shantanu invited every badge onto the atrium floor. No hierarchy, just fatigued smiles.

"We said transparency is velocity. Tonight you made us supersonic," he declared, handing Argent an acrylic star engraved "First to Breach the Wall—And Mend It."

A song blasted, samosa trays rolled, CNBC cameras turned for closing shots, and somewhere in darknet alleys a user named SpectreFox posted: "Glass thicker than expected. Retreat—reconvene."

Ripple Effects

Venture firms announced adoption of "open hackathon clauses."

Two industrial giants phoned Natasha for BharatVault licensing talks—security sells.

SEBI proposed a pilot program: voluntary livestream audits for listing fast-track.

Internal morale index hit all-time high: 9.4/10.

Compass Update

A third concentric circle illuminated 45°: Ethics Hackathon Complete. The infinity symbol now glowed with orbiting rings—transparency expanding, pulling more allies into its gravity.

Underneath, engineers chalked the night's credo:

IF MANY CAN SEE, FEW CAN SEIZE.

Shantanu pocketed the chalk, gaze climbing glass walls that no longer felt fragile but alive—mirrors on one side, shields on the other, windows for everyone willing to look in.

CHAPTER NINETEEN

Margins & Moats

The hackathon hangover still prickled everyone's eyelids when finance chief Gayatri hurled the next gauntlet:

"Great stories don't pay cloud bills. We need profit velocity—and we need it before the next fiscal closes."

The race to prove ethics could bankroll growth had begun.

1 ▪ The Three-Point Plan

- **Monetise the Glass** – Sell BharatVault as a compliance-first SaaS to every factory terrified by the new Patriot Act fines.
- **Exploit the Street Cred** – Use the EthicScore™ badge (born from the hackathon) to enter foreign markets that blacklist shady vendors.
- **Kill Silent Bleeds** – Eradicate every rupee of legacy waste hiding behind "that's how we've always done it."

Gayatri's eyes flashed toward Shantanu: "We built a moat of trust; now fill it with revenue deep enough for dragons to drown."

2 ▪ **Selling Daylight**

Natasha led a blitz dubbed Operation Lighthouse—no glossy decks, just livestream demos of BharatVault surviving red-team assaults. Within a month:

- Nine Fortune-500 suppliers signed pilot deals.
- A German auto-giant offered a € 12 million licence for Europe—provided data stayed inside the EU. Shreya cloned "EuroVault" in record time, code-reused at 82 %.
- A Southeast-Asian port signed after watching the ransomware livestream replay on YouTube.

Revenue curve bent like bamboo in monsoon.

3 ▪ The Streak of Lean Murder

Amit launched "Code or Close"—every dormant micro-service that hadn't shipped value in six months faced live tribunal. Engineers had to justify CPU cycles before a panel of peers and one sarcastic bot named Booly that reposted cost per user in chat.

Results:

- 38 services sunset, saving ₹4.6 crore annually.
- Shreya refactored telemetry pipelines, slicing cloud egress 27%.
- Employees coined a motto: "Murder scope, not engineers."

Morale rose; waistlines shrank with vanished late-night pizza budgets.

4 ▪ Street Smarts, Wall Street Numbers

Quarter-end arrived. Analysts packed the webcast expecting red ink. Gayatri strode on camera with the Compass Wall shimmering behind her:

- Top-line: +28% QoQ
- Gross margin: up from 38% to 46%
- Net profit: positive for the first time in nine quarters

She ended with two slides: a samosa emoji (for culture) and a lock emoji (for moat). Twitter lit: "Did SecuComp just invent ethical hyper-growth?"

Share price popped 18%—not a rocket, a steady lift like a 747 leaving runway, gear retracting with reassuring thunk.

5 ▪ Drama in the Wings

Success attracts imitators and saboteurs. SpectreFox re-appeared on darknet, promising "**Operation Prism Crack—shatter the moat.**" Investors asked if SecuComp could keep margins when security costs soared.

Dr Mira addressed a town hall:

"A moat isn't concrete; it's discipline. Dragons can fly. We'll keep stretching the moat until the wings tire first."

6 ▪ Moat-Measuring Day

Natasha staged an internal contest: teams pitched wild cost--saving or revenue-hacking ideas in three-minute TikTok-style clips. Winners:

- **Carbon Credit Arbitrage** – use predictive maintenance data to prove energy savings, sell credits on global exchanges; projected ₹15 crore yearly.
- **Ghost-Factory Guardian** – cheap sensor kit + BharatVault Lite for small manufacturers ignored by big vendors; blue-ocean market of 50,000 plants.

Gayatri green-lit both within 24 hours, crowning a new mantra: "Ship, Show, Share."

7 ▪ Investor Day—Full Circle

Twelve months after the first forged invoice exposé, SecuComp hosted analysts amid transparent server racks. No NDAs. Glass everywhere.

A senior fund manager whispered to Shantanu:

"We used to discount Indian tech for governance risk. Your compass changed our spreadsheet model."

That sentence was worth more basis points than any press headline.

8 ▪ Epilogue of the Quarter

Compass Wall gained a gold ring encircling the infinity symbol—the Margin Ring—etched with tonight's closing maxim:

INTEGRITY SCALES. EXCUSES DON'T.

The company toasted with filter-coffee, not champagne. Better margins.

Shantanu gazed at the glowing rings, realizing the moat was no ditch around the castle; it was the concentric circles themselves—each crisis faced, each line patched, each rupee earned without shadows. A living moat, expanding with every bright idea and every bright light.

Outside, storm clouds gathered; SpectreFox sharpened code. But inside SecuComp, daylight flooded hallways, reflecting off glass into eyes too awake to fear the dark

CHAPTER TWENTY

Prism Crack

SpectreFox's manifesto leaked on Pastebin at 02:34 IST:

"Glass cuts two ways.
We'll refract the light—turn your moat into a prism and crack the spectrum."

Unlike past stunt-hacks, this strike aimed at SecuComp's newest profit engine: Carbon-Credit Arbitrage—a platform certifying factories' energy savings, then selling those credits on the European ETS.

1 ▪ Anatomy of the Threat
Target Surface

- **Sensor Integrity** – falsify kWh readings → over-state carbon cuts → invalidate credits.
- **Ledger Manipulation** – inject ghost transactions on the blockchain side-chain.
- **Reputation Sabotage** – leak "fake credits" rumor before quarterly earnings.

Real-World Lesson:
Every new revenue stream is a new attack surface. CFOs must budget for security alongside product P&L—call it "Threat CAPEX."

2 ▪ Incident Day T-0
06:10 a.m. Pune plant's smart-meter data spiked 300% efficiency—impossible.
06:12 BharatVault's anomaly engine flagged "too good to be true."
06:15 Alert routed to Red-Team-On-Call (a rotation installed after the Ethics Hackathon).
06:25 Shreya froze carbon-credit issuance, triggering auto-notify to EU registry—pre-emptive disclosure before journalists could sniff.

Leader Takeaway:

Speed beats spin. Have pre-approved disclosure playbooks that ops can trigger without waiting for legal.

3 ▪ Digital Forensics Window

Within 90 minutes, Devika's team:

- Replayed signed sensor packets—discovered identical hash on two "different" meters → clone attack.
- Tracked clone to compromised Time-Sync daemon in a third-party IIoT gateway.
- Correlated anomaly IPs to a TOR exit node previously linked to a SpectreFox probe (from Hackathon logs).

Shantanu authorised "Open Forensics": a real-time Grafana board visible to EU regulators, Indian Ministry of Power, and customers. Hit count peaked at 42,000 viewers.

Leader Playbook Point:

Open forensics turns stakeholders into allies, crowdsourcing scrutiny that pressure-tests findings—and deters rumor-mills.

4 ▪ Containment & Counter-Narrative

08:00 Ops isolated affected gateways, switched plants to manual power-meter snapshots with union witnesses— physical verification foils data forgers.

10:30 Natasha hosted a joint press+union briefing on the factory floor—media filmed workers reading real meters, comparing to BharatVault dashboards.

13:00 EU registry issued in-principle statement: "We see no evidence credits in market are tainted."

Leadership Insight:

Front-line employees as credibility anchors: public trusts a wrench-holding technician more than a suit with a mic.

5 ▪ Root-Cause Sprint (48 h)

- Vendor firmware compiled with outdated OpenSSL → predictable PRNG → SpectreFox forged TLS sessions.
- Patch developed in 16 h, validated by two rival CTOs invited as neutral verifiers—competition converted to confidence.

SecuComp shipped a white-paper: "TLS Randomness Pitfalls in IIoT Gateways" under Creative Commons. Downloaded 80,000 times by week's end.

Lesson for Leaders:

Publish your scars; they become community armor and brand moat.

6 ▪ Strategic Aftershocks

* **Policy Win** – Indian Bureau of Energy Efficiency mandated real-time attestation protocols modelled on BharatVault.
* **Market Reward** – EU carbon desk increased purchase cap for SecuComp-verified credits by 20%.
* **Investor Signal** – Two ESG funds took positions, citing "robust integrity infrastructure."

Executive KPI Shift:

Added "Mean Time to Transparent Disclosure (MTTD)" as board metric.

Goal: < 30 minutes from anomaly detection.

7 ▪ Reflective Debrief

Board meeting minutes (publicly posted):

* "Every innovation invites infiltration; we must budget 'Integrity-Opex' equal to 5% of new-product revenue."
* "Security is marketing—Sunlight sells."
* "Partnership beats paranoia: involve competitors and regulators early."

Shantanu closed with a slide titled "Prism Principles":

Principle : Refract, Don't Distract

Pragmatic Action: Break attacks into public knowledge elements before rumor does.

Principle :Verify on the Ground

Pragmatic Action: Pair digital alerts with physical validation—human eyes, stamped logs.

Principle : Publish & Polinate

Pragmatic Action: Turn fixes into open standards; competitive advantage shifts to speed, not secrecy.

8 ▪ Maxim on the Compass Wall

A MOAT OF LIGHT ABSORBS NO SHADOWS

The Prism Crack failed; instead, it carved a clearer channel between SecuComp, regulators, and the factories they served. Margins held. Moat deepened—because every shard of attempted deceit was refracted back into collective learning.

C-Suite Cheat Sheet (for your own org):

- Allocate Threat CAPEX with every new product line.
- Embed Public Disclosure Triggers directly in incident-response runbooks.
- Use Employees as Evidence—front-line authenticity is PR money can't buy.
- Open-Source Post-Mortems to turn costs into communal capital.
- Measure MTTD (< 30 min)—because rumors travel at Wi-Fi speed.

SpectreFox retreated, but the reflection on the glass walls only grew brighter, blinding would-be intruders and lighting a road map for any leader with courage to walk it.

CHAPTER TWENTY-ONE

Funding the Beacon

Prism Crack proved SecuComp could survive a direct hit. Now Shantanu wanted more than survival; he wanted an industry immune-system. That meant turning the company's hard-won playbook into a **Beacon Standard**—open protocols, shared threat feeds, and a public-good fund that any manufacturer or vendor could tap.

The dream was noble.

The budget was brutal.

1 ▪ The Capital Conundrum

Gayatri's spreadsheet glared red:

Beacon rollout across South-Asia →   ₹240 crore over three years.

That rivalled R&D for two whole product lines.

Investors loved margins, not charity.

Regulators applauded, but had no chequebook.

Customers wanted the Beacon yesterday—"but please, don't raise prices."

Leadership Reality Check

Vision without funding is a LinkedIn post. Secure the runway, or the beacon never lights.

2 ▪ Three Financing Arrows

Beacon Bond – a sustainability-linked bond indexed to "Incidents Averted." Coupon drops 50 bps each quarter the Beacon database prevents a verified outage.

Moonshot Levy – 0.75 % surcharge on every BharatVault transaction, itemised on invoices as "Security Cooperative Fee." Opt-out allowed (public shaming likely).

Gov-Match Grant – ask Ministries of Commerce & Power to co-fund, rupee-for-rupee, any open-source security patch that clears three critical audits.

Shantanu told Gayatri: "One arrow may miss; three form a pattern investors can't ignore."

3 ▪ Investor Roadshow — With the Lights On

No mahogany boardrooms. Instead, Natasha livestreamed the pitch from the factory floor—sparks flying behind her.

Slide 1: cost of downtime in India's manufacturing sector → ₹ 19,000 crore/year

Slide 2: Beacon predicted to slash that by 8 % → ₹ 1,520 crore saved

Slide 3: Bond holders' variable coupon tied to verified savings.

Fund managers toggled calculators; risk analysts grinned—the bond's downside hedged by the very resilience it financed.

Leader Takeaway

Make investors partners in prevention, not mere spectators of growth.

4 ▪ The Price-Tag Debate

Customers balked at the Moonshot Levy—until Natasha published a dashboard comparing levy cost to historical ransomware losses. Average surcharge: ₹ 12,700/year; average ransom avoided per plant last year: ₹ 4.1 lakh.

Union leader Suresh recorded a 30-second video with a greasy wrench in hand:

"Twelve thousand buys peace of mind—and pays for itself the first time SpectreFox sneezes."

Video went viral; opt-outs dwindled to 2.6 %.

5 ▪ Regulatory Match

Shreya demoed Beacon's Patch-as-Policy pipeline to India's Minister of Power: zero-day disclosed → patch verified by dual auditors → pushed to all member factories in < 36 h.

Minister signed an MoU pledging ₹ 80 crore matching funds over two years.

Policy Hack

Tie government spending to measurable security SLAs; bureaucrats love dashboards more than brochures.

6 ▪ Closing the Round

- Beacon Bond oversubscribed 2.3× at a 5-year tenor.
- Moonshot Levy locked in ₹ 61 crore ARR.
- Gov-Match guarantee inked.

Total committed: ₹265 crore—Beacon fully funded with buffer for scope creep.

Compass Wall lit a new ring, indigo this time—Beacon Funded—and a maxim etched beneath:

BUILD WITH OTHERS' TRUST, PAY WITH YOUR OWN.

7 ▪ Operational Blueprint (Real-World Playbook)

Beacon's operational blueprint rests on five interlocking practices that any leader can replicate.

- First, the company publishes an open, real-time threat-intelligence feed—a public JSON stream of fresh indicators of compromise—because malware evolves by the hour and collective herd immunity is impossible if data is pay-walled.
- Second, it finances reliability with incident-indexed resilience bonds whose coupons fall whenever Beacon prevents an outage, turning investors into vocal advocates for rock-solid uptime.
- Third, security funding is embedded straight into revenue through a tiny, clearly itemised 0.75% "Security Co-op Fee" on every BharatVault transaction; most customers opt in once they realise the levy is cheaper than even one ransomware recovery.
- Fourth comes a dual-audit patch pipeline: every software fix is reviewed by two independent security firms, and their sign-offs, hashes, and test artefacts are written to an immutable ledger so regulators, clients, and journalists can verify that no shortcut was taken.

Finally, Beacon enlists the shop floor itself through union-championed advocacy—unions receive live dashboards and talking points, making them credible messengers who can defend Beacon's safeguards when a crisis hits.

Adopt these elements one at a time—publish a small feed, wire a micro-levy, or pilot dual audits—and you evolve from reactive patching to a self-financing, community-reinforced security culture that will outlive its founders.

Adopt one pillar, and your org levels up; adopt all five, and you become a lighthouse others steer by.

8 ▪ From Moat to Maritime Highway

Gayatri closed a global all-hands:

"The moat kept dragons out. The Beacon invites allies in, so the whole fleet sails safer."

Margins dipped 1.4% from the levy, then rebounded on new Beacon-tier contracts. Analysts updated models: "SecuComp morphing from product company to resilience platform—TAM up 3×."

9 ▪ Coda: SpectreFox's New Post

In a dark forum thread, SpectreFox wrote:

"They monetised sunlight. Interesting. Storms blot out sun; let's invent clouds."

Challenge accepted, Shantanu thought—because clouds pass, but beacons, once lit, guide through any weather.

CHAPTER TWENTY-TWO

Storm-Born Clouds

The Beacon's first threat blew in not through fiber, but through friendship.

1 ▪ Supply-Chain Sirens

One monsoon evening, Kavya's phone lit with a frantic message from **Varun Rao**, CEO of SkyBridge Hosting—a tiny Bengaluru cloud reseller that supplied edge nodes to dozens of Beacon factories.

"Our billing portal's gone. Ransom note demands 15 BTC. They claim to have Beacon VPN secrets. Help!"

SkyBridge was too small for 24×7 SOC coverage, too critical to ignore; its compromised jump-boxes could tunnel past the moat.

Leadership Lens

Your security perimeter ends where your smallest vendor's diligence begins.

2 ▪ The Social-Engineering Play

SecuComp's forensic team discovered the breach vector: a bogus LinkedIn request from a "Beacon Auditor" asking SkyBridge engineers to join a security Slack. The invite link delivered a payload exploiting an unpatched Electron vulnerability.

The sender's avatar? A stylised fox mask in pastel clouds.

SpectreFox had swapped zero-days for zero-trust gaps—in people.

3 ▪ Beacon in Action—First Live Drill

Shreya triggered Beacon Tier-2 Alert—supply-chain compromise:

1. Auto-Notify all member factories: switch VPN creds, restrict traffic from SkyBridge IP ranges.
2. Rapid Aid—deploy SecuComp's IR crew to SkyBridge at no cost (a Beacon pledge).
3. Crowd Pulse—publish IoCs (Indicators of Compromise) across Beacon feed within 30 minutes.

TTD (Time to Disclosure): 18 min.

Factories yanked access before attackers could pivot.

Real-World Takeaway

Incidents at partners must flow through the same public arteries as first-party breaches; delay equals contagion.

4 ▪ Contain-and-Coach

On-site, Devika found SkyBridge's backups intact but their encryption keys in plain text on a shared drive labeled "Lotsa Keys ??."

SecuComp's team rebuilt the portal in 9 hours, rotated every key, and—crucially—trained SkyBridge staff on secure secret management using **Vault-as-a-Service** (an open-source module Beacon had just released).

Varun signed an MOU to adopt Beacon's minimum-hygiene playbook; 11 other micro-vendors followed within weeks, lured by free tooling and the fear of public shame.

5 ▪ Metrics & Money

Beacon's dashboard showed:

- Supply-Chain Incident Averted: 1
- Factories Impacted: 0
- Average Vendor Onboarding Time: down from 14 days to 36 hours (thanks to pre-configured Vault module)

Analysts noted the moat expanding without bloating costs.

Gayatri's spreadsheet smiled: vendor churn decreased procurement overhead by ₹2.3 crore annually.

6 ▪ Culture Ripple—Security as Fellowship

Union leader Suresh recorded another viral clip, this time arm in arm with Varun:

"Big or small, we sink or sail together. Beacon is our life jacket."

The narrative shifted: not Big Brother SecuComp policing suppliers, but a fellowship where giants and garages shared the same flashlight.

7 ▪ SpectreFox's Weather Report

Minutes after Beacon's incident post-mortem went live, a new Pastebin surfaced:

"Clouds dissipate in wind. We will be the wind."

Shantanu wrote on the war-room whiteboard:

Next probable move: *phishing storms at scale—deep-fake voice calls, AI-generated invoices.*

Devika beneath it: *"Solution: authenticate intent, not identity—every payment, every patch."*

8 ▪ Compass Wall, New Layer of Glass

A translucent overlay appeared on the Compass Wall—Vendor Constellation—each dot a supplier, colour-coded by Beacon-compliance score. When SkyBridge's dot turned from amber to green during the town-hall, applause rolled like thunder.

Maxim etched for the day:

A CHAIN IS AS STRONG AS THE QUIETEST LINK.

9 ▪ Leadership Playbook—Storm Edition

- **Vendor-Zero Drills** – quarterly tabletop exercises that start with a random supplier, not HQ.
- **Public SLA for Aid** – promise IR help within 4 h to any compliant vendor; write it in contracts.
- **Human Patch Notes** – after each incident, share a 2-minute video explaining what people should do differently, not just systems.
- **Intent Authentication** – layered approvals tied to behaviour analytics, thwarting voice deep-fakes.
- **Constellation Dashboards** – visualise entire supply-chain hygiene; shame is a powerful disinfectant.

Adopt them, and you build an ecosystem umbrella, not just a corporate raincoat.

10 ▪ Coda: Funding Justified

A sceptical analyst asked on the next earnings call: "Beacon spend still rising; where's the ROI?"

Gayatri answered with one slide: "Zero production outages YTD despite three tier-2 threats. Estimated customer losses prevented: ₹280 crore. Beacon cost: ₹91 crore."

Silence, then: "Next question."

Margins safe, moat widening, Beacon bright. Storm-born clouds had tried to smother the light; instead, they illuminated every leak, every lesson, every small partner brought into the circle.

SecuComp braced for SpectreFox's wind, confident that a community bound by sunlight weathers any storm.

CHAPTER TWENTY-THREE

Wind Against the Glass

The first gust was a phone call that sounded exactly like Gayatri.

1 ▪ The Voice in the Wire

09:14 IST, Monday.

Accounts-payable clerk Reena answered a direct line—caller ID: "CFO Gayatri Iyer."

"Morning, Reena. I need an urgent wire— ₹4.7 crore to Eclipse Consulting,

invoice 8831-B. Board-approved. Send before noon, please."

Tone perfect. Cadence perfect. Only one tell: Gayatri never used please on money moves.

Reena stalled with a canned line from Beacon's new **Human Patch Notes #6:**

"Happy to, ma'am—just need the Compass Code first."

Click. Line went dead.

SpectreFox's wind had arrived: AI-generated voice-phishing, or vishing, scripted from hours of earnings-call audio.

Leader Insight

Attackers now clone authority, not credentials. Train staff to verify intent, not identity.

2 ▪ Beacon Tier-3: Authority Spoof

Within 30 minutes, four more Beacon companies reported similar calls—voices mimicking their own CFOs or CEOs, always requesting six-figure wires to "Eclipse Consulting."

Shreya escalated to Tier-3—network-wide threat:

- Freeze high-value wires pending secondary verification.

- Activate Behavioural Biometrics—pilot code that flags anomalies in speech patterns on corporate VoIP.
- Deploy Compass Code—a rotating 4-word pass-phrase (e.g., "orchid-salsa-hinge-29") required in all verbal financial approvals.

3▪Building the "Ear-Wall"
Behavioural Biometrics Stack

- **Voice-Print Delta** – compares live speech to baseline timbre + microsyllable signature.
- **Semantics Engine** – scans for politeness markers Gayatri never uses in directives.
- **Ledger Cross-Check** – queries ERP for matching invoice lineage in < 2 seconds.

Open-sourced as Ear-Wall v1.0 within 24 h; Beacon vendors could drop it into Asterisk or Zoom with a YAML config.

Implementation Note

Protective tech must be lightweight and shareable; complexity is the enemy of adoption.

4▪Live-Fire Drill—Stopping the Gusts

Day 2: SpectreFox's bots called 170 finance staff across the network. Ear-Wall flagged 164 as forgeries; six reached humans but failed Compass Code. Zero wires sent.

SpectreFox pivoted: deep-fake WhatsApp voice notes. Kavya's team rolled an update to verify **audio hash watermarks**—open standard from MIT Media Lab—within 48 h.

5▪Educating the Human Firewall

Rather than a dull memo, Natasha filmed a 90-second noir-style skit: a shadow figure mimicking Shantanu, foiled by a junior accountant wielding Compass Code.

Posted on Beacon feed, it racked up 60k views; suppliers begged to translate it into Hindi, Tamil, Bahasa.

Takeaway

Humans remember stories, not SOP PDFs. Make training binge-worthy.

6▪Quantifying the Wind

- Attempted fraudulent wires: ₹112 crore
- Funds lost: ₹0
- Ear-Wall deployment across Beacon: 82% in one week
- Average verification delay added to legitimate wires: 4 minutes

Finance chiefs accepted the lag; cost of trust < cost of breach.

7▪Boardroom Debrief – Redefining Trust

Dr Mira summarized:

"Identity can be forged; behaviour is harder. Trust henceforth is a pattern, not a person."

The board voted to embed behavioural analytics into every high-risk workflow—procurement, code-push, even press releases.

Gayatri joked: "If I ever say 'please' on a wire call again, block me—I've been hacked or I've found zen."

8▪Compass Wall—The Glass Flexes

A new swirl appeared around the Vendor Constellation—Ear-Wall Halo—symbolising acoustic defense. Below it, today's maxim:

THE STRONGEST GLASS BENDS WITH THE WIND.

9▪Playbook for Leaders—Wind Edition

- Multi-Factor AUTHORITY, not just authentication—tie approvals to unique speech or workflow style.
- Rotating Pass-Phrases for any voice-based orders; change daily, share via secure channel.
- Ear-Wall-As-Open-Source—security gains mass only when everyone can deploy.
- Micro-Drama Training—edutain, don't mandate, to engrain reflexes.
- Lag Budgeting—insert small, known friction into critical transactions; measure it like insurance.

Adopt these, and gusts of social engineering bounce off your glass walls instead of shattering them.

10▪SpectreFox Forecast

A fresh Pastebin note:

"Wind meets wall. Next, we seed the storm in the data itself."

Shantanu underlined data itself on the whiteboard—anticipating poisoned machine-learning models, manipulated carbon-sensor baselines.

The Beacon would need not just to defend glass but purify the water behind it.

SecuComp tightened bolts, confident the flexing glass could bear stronger winds—and readying to filter whatever stormy tide SpectreFox brewed next.

CHAPTER TWENTY-FOUR

Tainted Wells

SpectreFox no longer tried to smash the glass; it sought to poison the water it protected.

1 ▪ The Quiet Contamination

SecuComp's energy-efficiency A.I., Saffron, began predicting impossibly high savings for a cluster of Tamil Nadu textile mills. Numbers looked glorious—until on-site meters contradicted them.

Natasha sensed déjà vu. "Check the training logs," she told Kavya. Hours later they found it: a stealthy commit injecting 12 GB of synthetic sensor rows—perfectly formatted, subtly skewed upward.

The code signed off by an intern's stolen Git token four weeks prior. No alarm: hashes matched; tests passed. Data, unlike code, rarely triggers IDS.

Leader's Lesson

AI is a mirror of its data; smudge the mirror and decisions warp silently.

2 ▪ Beacon Tier-4 — Data Integrity Crisis

Tier-4, the highest alert, summoned regulators to the war room.

Action Grid:

- Freeze Saffron outputs—factory dashboards revert to raw meter readings.
- Trace Provenance—rebuild lineage from every CSV ingested since the intern's token breach.
- Deploy Canary Queries—statistical tests hunting improbable correlations (e.g., efficiency gains exactly matching power tariff hikes).

3 ▪ The Provenance Chain Project

Shreya unveiled a dormant R&D repo: **DataWell**—a blockchain-backed DAG recording every dataset's origin, checksum, and transformation script.

In 72 hours of caffeine-fueled sprinting, engineers wired DataWell into Saffron's pipeline, back-filling six months of lineage. Red nodes popped where synthetic data had entered—like blood spatter under UV.

They published the tooling under Apache 2.0; rival analytics firms forked it within a day.

Implementation Nugget

Treat data like code: version, review, sign. If your CI/CD ignores CSVs, attackers won't.

4 ▪ Purging the Poison

Affected Credits Frozen: € 11 million

Customers Informed: 27

Manual Audits Dispatched: 12 teams with portable calorimeters

Findings: actual efficiency unchanged. Credits would have been over-issued by 38%—a potential scandal dwarfing Prism Crack.

Saffron retrained on verified datasets; predictions normalised. Credits thawed after EU inspectors reviewed DataWell proofs.

5 ▪ Industry Shockwave

EU ETS issued guidance recommending **"cryptographic provenance chains"** for any AI-based credit claims—citing SecuComp's response as template.

Indian Institute of Corporate Affairs announced a workshop: "DataWell & the Future of Trustworthy AI." Registrations sold out in two hours.

ROI Snapshot

Beacon cost for DataWell sprint: ₹ 11 crore

Fines avoided: estimated € 45 million

New consulting pipeline for DataWell deployments: ₹ 60 crore projected ARR

6 ▪ Human Dimension—The Intern's Anguish

The intern, Arjun, hadn't gone rogue; his laptop was compromised at a café. Shantanu filmed a candid interview with him (after legal clearance):

"I thought pushing data was harmless; I never imagined my token could sink the whole ship."

Video released on Beacon feed, paired with guidelines on securing personal devices. View count: 1.2 million. Sympathy replaced scapegoating; education replaced blame.

7 ▪ Compass Wall—A Well of Light

A crystalline column animated on the Wall—DataWell Provenance—water flowing downward, arrows marking each transformation. The day's maxim surfaced like a koi:

CLEAN WATER, CLEAR VISION.

8 ▪ Leadership Playbook—Data Battlefield

- Sign & Version All Data—treat CSVs like binaries; mandate code-review-style sign-offs.
- Statistical Canary Tests—embed anomaly detection at ingest; math is the new IDS.
- Immutable Lineage Graphs—blockchain optional; transparency mandatory.
- Shared Tooling—open-source your provenance stack; community eyes catch what logs miss.
- Culture of Custodianship—train every data handler, from intern to C-suite, as guardians of the well.

Adopt these, and poisoned wells become clear fountains—visible, verifiable, vital.

9 ▪ SpectreFox's Murmur

A terse dark-forum post:

"Water purified. Next we tilt the compass."

Shantanu circled the word compass—preparing for attacks on the very trust dashboard that had become Beacon's pulse.

Glass, wind, water—now magnetism. SecuComp's journey turned elemental, each threat refining another virtue, each defense published as a roadmap for leaders who dared transparency.

CHAPTER TWENTY-FIVE

Magnetic Drift

SpectreFox understood symbols move markets faster than exploits.
If the Compass Wall could no longer be trusted, every maxim, metric, and morale boost would crumble.

1 ▪ The Subtle Skew

It began with a barely-noticeable anomaly: Beacon uptime tickers showed 99.72 %, when Gayatri's raw logs said 99.89 %. Only two-hundredths off—small enough to dodge dashboards, large enough to seed doubt.

Shreya's team verified the API: pristine. Yet the Wall's front-end displayed the crooked figure. Someone wasn't hacking the data; they were tilting the needle we relied on to read it.

Leadership Truth

Attackers don't always steal or smash—they distort, eroding confidence atom by atom.

2 ▪ Hunting Phantom Fields

Devika traced display code commits; nothing malicious. Next, they packet-captured the Wall's WebSocket feed—clean. Finally, Kavya instrumented browser memory on the Wall's kiosk PC.

There it was: a side-loaded Chrome extension named "MoatTheme Enhancer" injecting a JavaScript routine that shaved metrics with a random negative bias between 0.1–0.3 %.

Installed manually. On CCTV, a night-shift janitor paused, wiped the screen...and plugged in a USB. Face obscured by cap. Badge—a vendor cleaner contracted last month.

SpectreFox had gone physical.

3 ▪ Compass Tier-X Response

New protocol—Tier X—for symbol tampering:

- **Hardware quarantine**—replace kiosk PCs; isolate USB for forensics.
- **Metric Integrity Audit** —cross-validate every historical value against signed logs.
- **Symbol Authentication**—digitally sign visual assets; kiosk verifies signature before render.

4 ▪ Forensic Findings

USB payload contained:

- The Chrome extension.
- A slow-burn worm seeking any display tied to SecuComp offices.
- Instructions labelled "Project Gyroscope"—goal: "Induce perception of slow decay → investor flight."

The janitor? A subcontractor hired via a shell facility-services firm traced to Dubai—same PO box tied previously to SpectreFox cryptowallets.

Leader's Wake-Up

The supply chain of custodial staff is part of your security perimeter.

5 ▪ Securing Symbols—The Trust Overlay

Shreya and Natasha launched **TrustOverlay**:

- **Signed SVG Layer**—all metrics rendered server-side into a hashed SVG, verified in kiosk via TPM chip.
- **Laser-Etched Physical Seal**—Compass Wall glass now embedded with nano-QR linking to a public hash; any replacement panel would expose mismatch.
- **Citizen Verify App**—any visitor can scan the Wall with AR to see real-time metric hash vs blockchain ledger.

Open-sourced, of course. A museum in Tokyo adopted it for art provenance within a week.

6 ▪ Communications Counter-Strike

Rather than hush the drift, Shantanu held a livestream titled "How We Almost Lied To Ourselves." He walked viewers through the exploit, demoed the corrupted extension, then unveiled TrustOverlay live.

Viewers: 210,000.

Investor Q&A concluded with fund manager Tara Liang:

"If you can sign glass, we can sign term sheets."
SecuComp stock closed up 3%.

7▪Metrics Restored, Confidence Upgraded

Compass Accuracy Audit: 100% alignment restored.
Time to Detect Symbol Skew: 19 hours → new SLA target: 2 hours.
Number of external orgs cloning TrustOverlay within 30 days: 37.

8▪Playbook for Leaders—Symbol Security

- **Sign Your Dashboards**—cryptographic proof that visuals mirror source.
- **Zero-Trust Facilities**—vet janitorial, signage, and kiosk vendors as rigorously as pen-testers.
- **Public Verification Tools**—empower outsiders to validate your metrics; crowdsourced honesty multiplies trust.
- **Incident Transparency**—show the exploit live; candor converts scandal into brand equity.
- **Set Symbol-Tamper KPIs**—monitor time-to-detect visual drift just like MTTR for servers.

Adopt these and your strategic north star stays true even when saboteurs spin hidden magnets.

9▪Compass Maxim—Etched in Nano-Glass

WHEN THE NEEDLE HOLDS TRUE, STORMS ONLY PROVE THE COURSE.

The glass glowed brighter, its direction now verifiable by any passer-by with a phone. SpectreFox's gyroscope spun in vain; the compass corrected itself in public view.

10▪SpectreFox's Last Missive

Pastebin entry:

"Needles fixed, wells clean, wind blocked, glass bends. We tried. Your beacon blinds. New game: if we can't break you, we'll become you."

Shantanu smiled—an homage or a threat? Either way, transparency had turned attacks into advertisements. The final battle wouldn't be defense; it would be adoption.

CHAPTER TWENTY-SIX

Shadow Allies

The email arrived on Shantanu's private proton inbox—a single-sentence proposal signed "SpectreFox Ops":

"Let's license Beacon together—sunlight scales faster with two suns."

No threats, no riddles. A business offer.

1 ▪ The Temptation of Scale

Gayatri's back-of-napkin math:

Beacon deployed across SecuComp network = 4,200 factories.

SpectreFox's rumored clientele in Eastern Europe & Africa = 15,000 sites.

Licensing at even ₹8 lakh per site = ₹1,200 crore ARR.

Margins and moats shivered in anticipation.

Leadership Dilemma

When your adversary adopts your values—is it conversion or corruption?

2 ▪ Due-Diligence in the Dark

Natasha met SpectreFox under the safest conditions she could create: a spare room, a laptop that had never touched the internet, and every camera and microphone switched off. On the screen the SpectreFox people kept their faces blurry and their voices distorted—still half in the shadows.

Their offer came with three promises:

- No access to Beacon's inner workings: They would get only the ready-made software, not the source code they could tamper with.
- All money flows on the blockchain: Every rupee earned would move through a public smart-contract so regulators and journalists could see the split in real time.
- Shared security oversight: A joint council—SecuComp, SpectreFox, and outside experts from the EU—would take turns chairing and signing off every update.

Then their first slide flashed a cheeky line:

"Keep your friends close—and your enemies profitable."

The message was clear. SpectreFox believed that once both sides made money together, sabotage would cost too much. Natasha understood the risk: this was high-stakes diplomacy with yesterday's attackers, held together by open ledgers, rotating watchdogs, and a motto that warned her to stay alert even while shaking hands.

3 ▪ Boardroom Cleavage

Faction A – The Expansionists

"Adoption trumps vendetta. If SpectreFox monetises ethically, attacks stop by default."

Faction B – The Guardians

"Trust is brittle. Handing keys to yesterday's saboteur invites inside jobs."

Dr Mira proposed a third path: **"Sunlight Franchise"**—Beacon-lite APIs, stripped of core telemetry, governed by an independent public foundation.

4 ▪ Foundation Blueprint

- **3-Key Governance** —SecuComp, SpectreFox, and a neutral NGO each hold shard keys; any two can sign protocol updates.
- **Code in the Commons** —all non-security-critical modules MIT-licensed.
- **Global Auditathons** —annual bounty events where hackers earn equity in the foundation for finding flaws.
- **Ethics Escrow** —percentage of royalties routed to victims of past SpectreFox exploits until compensation pool hits ₹100 crore.

Gayatri's spreadsheet renamed revenue to "Redemption Yield."

5 ▪ Negotiation Chess

SpectreFox balked at Ethics Escrow. Shantanu counter-offered live on the blurred call:

"You poisoned wells; now sell filters. Escrow is price of entry."

After 48 silent hours, SpectreFox agreed—adding a clause: If any Beacon data is weaponised by state actors, escrow resets to zero. A hedge against geopolitical blowback.

6 ▪ Public Reveal—The Sunlight Summit

In a glass auditorium, Shantanu and an anonymous, hooded SpectreFox envoy signed digital contracts on Ledger wallets projected overhead. QR codes let viewers verify the transaction hash on-chain in real time.

Twitter hashtags exploded: **#BeaconPact #SunlightScales.**
Skeptics cried whitewash; supporters hailed pragmatic peace.

7 ▪ Early Wins & New Risks

Two months later:

- 2,300 SpectreFox-client factories onboarded; reported cyber incidents down 63 %.
- Ethics Escrow reached ₹ 12 crore.
- One auditathon uncovered a privilege-escalation bug—patched in 22 hours, bounty paid in equity.

But intelligence briefings warned: rival dark-net groups see Beacon's openness as exploitable map. Glass walls shine; they also outline.

Leader Insight

Transparency arms the good—and signals the bad. Mitigate by shortening detection loops, not by dimming the light.

8 ▪ Compass Wall—Twin Suns Motif

A second luminary icon lit beside the Beacon rings. Below, the maxim:

THE BRIGHTEST ALLIES ARE FORGED FROM FORMER SHADOWS.

Employees cheered. Investors hedged. Competitors scrambled to draft their own sunlight charters.

9 ▪ Playbook: Partnering with Ex-Adversaries

- **Convert Conflict into Contracts** —codify redemption in code and capital.
- **Tri-Stake Governance** —no duo can hijack without the third.
- **Victim Compensation First** —trust begins with restitution.
- **Equity-for-Bug Bounties** —align hacker incentives with platform health.
- **Dynamic Transparency** —broadcast hashes and escrows; conceal exploit vectors until patched.

Execute these, and yesterday's war becomes tomorrow's joint venture—with the public holding both parties accountable.

10 ▪ SpectreFox Epilogue—A Name Reborn

SpectreFox issued a statement:

"We retire the mask; we adopt the mirror. Our new name: GlassFox, reflecting all."

Whether a true metamorphosis or a tactical chrysalis, the industry now watched a living experiment: could a predator pivot to protector without shedding its cunning?

Shantanu knew the saga wasn't over. Trust is rented, never owned, and the rent is paid daily in disclosures, audits, and the gleam of uncompromised glass.

CHAPTER TWENTY-SEVEN

Eternal Lease

Beacon's reach now spanned five continents, 21,000 factories, and—through GlassFox—an unlikely fellowship of former foes.

Yet the larger Beacon grew, the louder one question echoed in policy blogs, boardrooms, and hacker forums alike:

Who owns the sun once it lights every street?

1▪The Fork Proposal

A coalition of civic technologists, ESG megafunds, and worker unions tabled an audacious motion:

Turn Beacon into **SOL-DAO**—a fully decentralised, token-governed public utility.

- Token-weighted votes would steer roadmap, bug-bounty budgets, and escrow distributions.
- SecuComp and GlassFox together would hold < 15% of governance tokens.
- Core protocol keys burned; upgrades possible only via on-chain consensus.

Shantanu saw liberation. Gayatri saw loss of monetisable IP.

GlassFox saw immortality without dependence on SecuComp's board.

2▪The Great Convocation

A hybrid summit convened in Bengaluru's Palace Grounds—12,000 in-person delegates, 90,000 in the metaverse twin.

Stage centre: The Beacon Key—three titanium shards set to meld in a plasma forge if DAO won the vote, symbolising irreversible decentralisation.

Debaters:

- **Gayatri Iyer** – "Keep stewardship; Wall Street still funds sunlight."
- **Dr Mira Parikh** – "Governance by many or trust in none—your choice."
- **GlassFox envoy** – mask replaced by clear visor—"Predators cannot be landlords of the light they once hunted."
- **Union leader Suresh** – "Workers deserve a literal stake; give us tokens, not platitudes."

Streams lit up with sentiment analyses: 68 % pro-DAO after first day.

3 ▪ Crunching the Consequences

Scenario A – Corporate Beacon

- + Stable revenue forecasts.
- – Growing antitrust scrutiny: two private firms steering global audit rail.
- – GlassFox credibility questioned every quarter.

Scenario B – SOL-DAO

- + Unassailable transparency; regulators endorse, don't enforce.
- + Token grants crowd-fund perpetual R&D.
- – Possible governance gridlock; upgrades pace uncertain.
- – SecuComp revenue hit—licensing shifts to protocol fees capped by DAO.

Kavya built a Monte Carlo model: long-run NPV nearly identical—corporate moat versus DAO network effect balanced out.

4 ▪ The Vote

Token distribution airdropped one week prior:

- 30 % to active Beacon nodes (factories & vendors).
- 15 % to workers via union rosters.
- 15 % to security researchers with prior bug-bounty contributions.
- 25 % reserved treasury for future adopters.
- 15 % split between SecuComp and GlassFox.

Quorum threshold: 67 %.
Vote window: 48 hours, blockchain-recorded.

Final tally streamed live on Compass Wall—now itself signed by the provisional DAO contract.

YES (fork to DAO): 71.4%

NO: 28.6%

Applause thundered; plasma forge ignited, fusing shards into an amber ingot—keys melted, control ceded.

5▪Corporate Sunset, Community Dawn

Gayatri issued a press release within the hour:

"We built the Beacon. Now the world holds the lease. SecuComp will innovate at protocol edges, compete on service, and answer to the same sunlight as everyone else."

GlassFox tweeted a single line:

"We are all custodians now."

Stock markets wobbled, then stabilised as analysts rerated SecuComp from "platform owner" to "premium node operator" with sticky expertise.

6▪Governance Genesis Block

Block 0 of SOL-DAO engraved:

SUNLIGHT SURVIVES ITS PIONEERS.

Follow-up proposals flooded in:

- #3 – Fund academic fellowships on data-lineage research.
- #7 – Equip sub-Saharan clinics with free Beacon nodes.
- #12 – Annual "Spectre Grants" to white-hat teams, reclaiming a name once feared.

Tokens shifted, discussions burned bright—democracy at algorithmic speed.

7▪Leadership Epilogue—Lessons for Eternity

- **Design for Dispossession** – if a system can't outlive its founders, it was never big enough.
- **Profit to Prototype, Purpose to Perpetuate** – corporate capital births tools, but public stewardship sustains them.
- **Transparency Is a Ratchet** – once cranked, it rarely turns back.
- **Adversaries Are Unpaid Auditors** – engage, convert, and ultimately enfranchise them.

- **Lease of Trust Renews Daily** – whether under a logo or a DAO, disclosure remains the rent.

8 ▪ Shantanu's Quiet Moment

Late night, empty office. The Compass Wall—now just a node monitor—reflected Shantanu's faint smile.

From bootstrap bravado to Beacon DAO, his journey proved that risk, redemption, and relentless openness could turn even corporate glass into a community constellation.

He whispered the final maxim, etched not on glass but in memory:

"Let there be light—and let it belong to all."

Epilogue

When Beacon ignited, its light was meant to guard a single company's perimeter. What followed instead was a decade-long experiment in radical transparency—one that rewrote the rules of corporate resilience, investor behaviour, and even organised labour. Looking back, the early crises feel almost quaint: phantom invoices, deep-fake phone calls, poisoned datasets. Each attack tested a pane of the expanding glass; each defense forced SecuComp to open another door until secrecy itself became the enemy.

Today, the SOL-DAO ledger hums quietly beneath everyday life. Factory operators in Coimbatore, regulators in Brussels, and security researchers in Nairobi all query the same open graph to validate uptime, patch provenance, or the escrow balance that still compensates victims of SpectreFox's darker years. Shantanu now chairs the DAO's rotating Ethics Council only once every thirty-six months—just another token holder among millions—while SecuComp thrives as a premium node operator competing on service, not monopoly. GlassFox, reborn from its predatory past, runs the largest bug-bounty accelerator on the network; its former exploits now case studies in the curriculum it funds.

The transformation has not been without tension. Governance votes stall, token prices swing, and hostile states occasionally probe the consortium's open APIs hoping to game the very sunlight that blinds them. Yet every attempt to weaponise transparency has so far been met with faster patches, wider disclosure, and new maxims etched on kiosks from São Paulo to Seoul: "Visibility breeds responsibility," "Trust is rented, payable daily."

What, then, of the future? Two proposals loom on the DAO forum. The first would seed Beacon nodes on low-Earth-orbit satellites, ensuring threat data flows even when terrestrial grids are silenced by disaster. The second seeks to integrate behavioural-biometric proofs into national ID programs, a step critics call intrusive and champions deem overdue. The debate is fierce, public, and—crucially—recorded forever on-chain. Whatever course is chosen, it will be visible to anyone with a browser and the curiosity to look.

Perhaps that is the lasting legacy: not any single policy or piece of code, but a cultural ratchet that refuses to turn backward. Founders now launch startups with open ledgers from day one, investors demand resilience clauses before they discuss valuation, and unions sit at the same security briefings as boards. The glass has bent so many times it has become a lens—magnifying every flaw yet focusing collective will to correct it.

If a single lesson endures, it is this: power hoarded turns brittle, but power illuminated becomes renewable. Beacon's founders expected to guard a castle; instead, they helped light a commons where even former adversaries take a shift at the watch. The sunlight, at last, belongs to all—and each dawn renews the eternal lease.

www.ingramcontent.com/pod-product-compliance
Lightning Source LLC
Chambersburg PA
CBHW040122150726
48005CB00015B/2326